The Gang-War

A work of fiction by Andy Gilbert

Preface & Warning

I have the utmost respect for the Police and the work they do under the most trying circumstances throughout NZ and I really should emphasise that any similarity to any person living or dead, in this novel, is a sheer coincidence.

Further I should add that I have based this story in Rotorua as it is a town I know well. The story could be based in any town or city around New Zealand and I would go to great lengths to emphasize that comment.

Copying and using

The writer specifically cancels any reproduction in part or in whole of this work. Any such permission needs to have been given in writing by the Author and at all times the copyright of this work is retained by the Author.

Table of Contents

Other work by the same Author

Chapter 1

I think it was a Thursday afternoon when I got the call.

It would have been just after 4.30pm as I was thinking about getting ready to go home for the day.

It was the Boss that called.

"It's happening. Ronnie has been shot at. You get up to the A&E ward and I will go and see Tohi. Let's see if we can get this one over before it starts!"

With that he closed his phone off and I was left staring at my phone while I thought about what he had just said.

"It's starting." What the hell did he mean by that?

Then as I replayed the conversation in my head, his next words hit home. "Ronnie has been shot".

The only Ronnie I know is Ronnie the head of the Mongrel mob in town. That can't be good.

Already I was heading out to my car and I should have said something to the Sarge.

Arriving at the A&E entrance at the hospital I hurried in. I wasn't worried about my vehicle being parked in a no parking zone. I had more important stuff to deal with! I hurried into the A&E where I was told they were admitting Ronnie and he had gone up to the ward. The nurse also asked me if I could do anything about the bodyguards that had appeared. I was already on my way up to the surgical ward so I didn't actually listen to what the nurse said.

When I got out of the lift at the third floor I was briefly examined by a gang member and deemed to be a civilian so I hurried into the ward. There was an argument going on halfway down the ward between two gang members and a nurse. I skirted my way past them and entered Ronnie's room.

Ronnie as usual had a big grin on his face, "Hey, Sarge. What, no grapes?"

I held out my hand to greet him but as he had a drip in his right arm and a huge gauze pad on his left arm, it wasn't reciprocated. He looked like he was in some pain but he still had his usual grin for me.

"Can I ask what the hell happened?" I asked him.

"Not my fault, Sarge. I'm just going home to my place and a shot comes from my left. Sounded like a rifle but my bike makes a lot of noise, so I can't really say. Next thing I know my left arm is buggered and I am steering with just my right and getting the hell out of there. I pulled up maybe 100 meters down the road and two of my lads are around me with their pistols out and covering me."

"Any damage?"

"Not to the bike and that's a plus. I've had that for five years and it's never given me an ounce of trouble."

"Not to the bike. What about you?"

"Me? Oh, yeah. Broken humerus. They reckon the bullet went clean through the bone. They reckon it will make the thing harder to heal. Something about the bone not having a clean surface to knit to. Oh, you can get that off the nurse probably with you being the law and stuff. Anyway the doc reckons they will have to put a plate in to get the bones to knit together. Reckons I could be in here for up to four days, and the nurse is getting a bit lippy about the boys being up here for my protection."

"Can I ask if you have anyone in mind for this?"

"Got to be Tohi, eh? They're getting a bit frisky and nudging us out of our patches. You know, dealing to those guys we have always dealt with. It's only a matter of time before he gets brave enough. He's been recruiting like mad. Reckons they have around 20 new members.

If that's right, they're nearly as strong as us. Looks like I might have to call in a few of the lads from Tauranga."

"Ronnie, the DI is meeting with Tohi as we speak. Are we going to have a war?"

"Depends if I take this as personal."

He thought for all of two seconds.

"Yeah, it's personal. Might be time to get the lads together and do some planning. Sarge, You know I can't let this one go."

"Ronnie. Let me and DI talk this one through. Give me 48 hours. Call it a truce or a ceasefire or whatever you want to call it."

"I'll give you 24 hours. Maybe we will meet and talk it through. Maybe I'll do some personal stuff. But I will give you 24 hours to get back to me. Fair enough?"

"I'll be up to see you by this time tomorrow," was my parting shot.

Ronnie's parting shot was more succinct, "Hey Sarge. Grapes would be nice!

Chapter 2

I rang the Boss. He said he would meet me back in the office as soon as I could get there.

I was into the office at 5.10 pm and the Sarge was still there and waiting for me.

"Well, have we got a gang war brewing?" was the Sarge's first question.

"Dunno. Where is the Boss?"

"In his office he's been there for ten minutes and on the phone to someone."

"It can't be anyone important enough to stop for a few moments." This was said as I was walking towards the Boss's office.

Behind me I heard the CI's voice, " Well if I am not important enough, I can assume you must have something to say about the matter."

Oh hell, now we had the big Boss in the meeting that's all I needed to make my day.

I stood back and allowed the big Boss to grab the best chair in the Boss's office. I grabbed the other chair and the Sarge stood behind me to get an idea of what was going down.

The Boss started with," I spoke to Tohi. He reckons it's just a coincidence that someone shot at Ronnie. Says it had nothing to do with him or the Black Power."

The big Boss interrupted, "And you, of course, believed him?"

"Course I bloody didn't. He's guilty as sin and he's also looking very smug. As if he knows something we don't."

I thought it was safe to put in my bit, "I've just been to see Ronnie. He's in a surgical ward and they will have to put a plate in to get the bones to knit. He says he has to take it personally, and he also reckons Tohi is behind it. If it was down to me, I reckon we have the makings of a gang war."

The big Boss was thinking out loud. "If we have a gang war it won't be pretty. Some of the gangs will go down but there is always the chance of civilians getting caught in the middle. This will do us no good in the papers."

My Boss was looking a little incredulous. "You're worried about how the papers will see it. Sorry about this but that's the least of my worries. If you hadn't noticed I have a bloody gang war breaking out in our patch!"

The big Boss looked contrite, "Sorry, Colin, I was thinking out loud and of course I'm worried about this gang war. I just have to look at the bigger picture. You know how the papers will treat it if we can't control it. Maybe I'll just sit still and listen to what I can. Sergeant, you were around in 05 or 06 when it last happened. How do you reckon this will pan out?"

The Sarge would have preferred to not say anything but as he had been asked directly he offered, "I dunno, Drive by Shootings. Perhaps a few executions of the gangs by the gangs, I'm guessing a bit of terror introduced into the neighborhoods to get the good folks of our town screaming for a stop to the killings. A stern letter from the Council telling us to do our job. Maybe a few acts of bravado where the gangs set up on one side of town or the other and we have a demarcation line. Black Power on one side and Mongrel Mob on the other side."

Realising he may have gone too far; the Sarge halted his speech. It was obvious he had more to say about a gang war but felt he had said enough.

The Boss chirped up, "And that is if it's a good war between Ronnie and the Black Power. If it gets dirty then both sides will fight dirty and we won't know where the next hit is coming from. Look. Let's meet here in the morning at 8.30 and we can have a think about any possibilities between now and then."

He looked at the big Boss, "That okay with you?"

"How about you and the lads meet and one of you get back to me. I have nothing to add. Maybe I'll get onto division and see if they have any ideas."

With that the meeting broke up. I walked with the Boss out to his car. His comment was to the effect that, "Shit, this could get messy, if it plays out!"

Friday

In at my usual time and the weather was promising to be a really nice day. I sat down with the Sarge and we spoke for a few minutes about what was likely to happen if the gangs did start a war. The Sarge had told me it got very messy in Rotorua when they last had a war. Now I looked back on it I spent the better part of 05, 06 and 07 in Napier. It's a thing that when you rise to a Senior Constable you jump ship for a year or two. Because I had served in Britain, I was allowed to do my Senior Constable exam quite early. I think they stopped that after I took my exam. I did my thing in Napier and a great time I had down there. The Sarge told me about some of the things they got up to, to countermand the gangs and their activities. With the newest sets of laws you would not get away with half of the stuff they got away with 18 or so years ago. Some say the crims have it all on their side and we do have to be so much more careful when we present a case to the Crown Prosecutor, nowadays.

That aside, the Sarge told me about some of the things that happened in '05. Drive by shootings. Blasting a house with a shotgun through the window and not worrying whether there were kids in the bedrooms. This was odd, because they were not inclined to get civilians involved in their war. Usually civilians were excluded from any retribution. In one instance the Sarge mentioned a case where one gang carried out a gangland style execution on a guy having a quiet drink at the pub. It got very messy and very bloody. I asked how did it all come to an end, the gang war and the Sarge just reckoned it stopped one day. It was as if the gangs had had enough and by agreement they just stopped the fight and did their own thing as if nothing had happened in the previous month or so.

I had already rung the hospital to find out how Ronnie was doing. It seems that they had operated on Ronnie the previous evening and put the plate in to aid the bone mending. The rest of the gang members wanted him to go home but one nurse had the guts to put her foot down and Ronnie had stayed in hospital overnight. He was still dozy from the anesthetic so she had stood up to the gang lads and said he wasn't going anywhere. I find it funny that a fully patched gang member will bow down to a woman in authority if she insists. The Boss told me later that it's a throwback to doing what your mother told you to do when you were a kid. That's one of the reasons why 'the little woman' can often hold so much power in the relationship. He did say more but I was wondering why that was and recalling my own childhood I thought he had it spot on.

The Boss called a meeting for everybody at 8.30am. Even Tim Cross was there! We had lost Dave Powell to Invercargill and in return we had got Bernie McDowell. She was proving to be useful as she already had her Senior Constable exam and she was a good source of reference for the new lads.

The Boss called the meeting to order by simply saying, "Right, you lot!"

Then he continued. He told us all what had happened to Ronnie and then he asked me for my input as to Ronnie's state of mind. When I said he had to take it personally, Tim and Mike groaned as they had an idea of what it would mean.

Then the Boss told how us he had met with Tohi the other gang leader. He went on to say that Tohi looked smug. "Bloody smug" was how the Boss described his attitude. As far as the Boss was concerned Tohi had organised the hit on Ronnie and he regarded Tohi as being 'cunning', so he would likely have a backup plan'. Our entire plan to ward off the inevitable gang war was based on me asking Ronnie to hold off any retaliation for twenty four hours until we got back to speaking to Ronnie. The Boss's final comment was to the effect of "So what do we get the DS say to Ronnie to avoid an all-out gang war. Any ideas?"

Nobody initially had anything to say then the suggestions started to flow. Although with each suggestion I knew we had a major problem on our hands.

'Arrest Tohi!'

"On what charge?"

"Anything that will get him off the street."

"Littering? We have as much chance arresting Tohi and his brief not getting him sprung within five minutes as I do of winning Britain's Got Talent."

Once the Boss started with the funnies I knew to shut the hell up. Derek hadn't reached my level of awareness with the Boss, yet.

"You could always arrest Ronnie."

"And when I get to the final of 'Britain's Got Talent' I thought I would give my version of Pok Areana. Come on lads, let's get real! Derek, perhaps we arrest Ronnie on a charge of, I dunno, stopping a bullet from going on its own sweet way maybe."

"What does a gang war involve?" asked someone.

The Sarge replied, "It's trouble with one of them capital letters. Last time we had a gang war there were shootings on the street, a demarcation line across town where the other gang were warned not to cross, random shootings where a civilian or a copper could get knocked over and killed. That's the good bit. Now we have all of this internet and stuff there is all of the hacking where you don't know where the truth lies. You get a message about a hit and you might be getting yourself lined up for an ambush."

The Boss cut the Sarge off," Yeah, thanks, Sarge. That's what we need. A good bit of morale boosting. That should do the trick!"

The Sarge looked as if he could have said more but he would keep it under his hat for a while. To tell the truth he looked teed off at the Boss.

"DS, when are you going up to see Ronnie?"

"This afternoon if we have nothing to talk to him about before?"

The Boss thought for a moment before he replied, "No, go up and see him now. Tell him you want to do an analysis of forensics. Say you want his bike and his jacket. Tell him you are still working on Tohi to call a truce. Say anything you want but delay any start to the war. Got it?"

"I've already told him you went to see Tohi yesterday."

"Just get the hell up to his hospital ward and talk him out of a retaliatory strike." That was the Boss's final comment for me.

"Mike, you and Derek get up to the Mob place on View Road. Keep a watch on anyone going in or out. You can't be everywhere so get me a list of number plates. I want to know who is going in and out of the Mob HQ. Bernie you and the Sarge dig out any info you can on the last time we had a gang war. Tim, you are up to speed with everything. You will maintain the night shift until I come up with anything better. So what are you all waiting for?"

With that I left the office and went to see Ronnie. Derek and Mike took up a patrol outside the Mongrel mob HQ on View Road. Bernie and the Sarge went looking for anything on the last time we had a gang war. The Boss went up to see Tohi.

I drove up to the hospital and parked where I had parked yesterday. Going up to the surgical ward I was not surprised to see a couple of Ronnie's lads outside his door. One of them I knew vaguely so he gave me a nod and allowed me to walk into Ronnie's room.

When I walked into Ronnie's room he was back to his jokey self, "Well, Sarge, I can't see you holding any bloody grapes so you must mean business. What can I do for you?"

"How're you feeling, Ronnie?"

"Not too bad. I reckon the drugs they give out here are as good as the stuff we sell and you can get them on a prescription. How're you doing?"

I was looking at Ronnie's face. He looked a bit ashen as if he was in some pain but did not want to let on about it. Maybe it was the painkillers he was on.

"Well, the Boss has got his knickers in a knot. Reckons we have the makings of a gang war on our hands. I told him you're too smart for that and it's bad for business."

"Sorry, Sarge. It has to be personal with Tohi and me. Worst case scenario, you might only have one gang to deal with. Best case scenario. Er... well, you might only have one gang to deal with."

That was not the answer I wanted to hear but it was the best I was going to get from Ronnie while he was in a hospital bed. "Ronnie, I'm going to need your jacket and your bike so we can do forensics on them. How do I get hold of them?"

"Jacket is in the cabinet there. I'm told I was quite insistent on them not cutting the jacket off. They reckon I pulled the jacket off rather than let them cut it. I have to respect the patch, even when I have had it for twenty years. Bike should be back at View Road. Someone else rode it back there. I don't reckon it got hit by a bullet but it should still be there in the garage below. How did your boss get on with Tohi?"

"Boss reckons he denied everything but I was having a word with the Boss afterwards and he reckons Tohi is too smart not to have another plan in place. I'm saying this so you keep your guard up. I can't afford to have to break in a new leader after I've put so much work into you."

Ronnie chuckled at my remark but I could see he was in some pain so I said a few more nice things and left him alone. I did ask the gang members outside when Ronnie could expect to go home. The nurse was passing by and she said four days. After she had gone the gang member whispered they reckon four days but they don't allow smokes in here so I reckon Ronnie will home by tomorrow. I took that as three days. Ronnie did like a fag now and then. Especially when he had to do some thinking, like today!

Oh and Ronnie asked me to check his bike out at the gang HQ. He reckoned if I left it for a day they would manage to hide anything they didn't want the cops to see. For me I reckoned he was still a little high from the drugs he was on. But I did agree to leave it for a day.

I had grabbed Ronnie's jacket from his hospital bedside cabinet and took it back to the labs for testing. I left it with them and reported back to the Boss.

"Ronnie is still convinced it was Tohi that set up the hit on him, and he still reckons he will have to do something about Tohi. He can't let this one go, so it looks like we still have a potential gang war on our plate."

The Boss looked a little rueful as he said, "I had a word with Tohi this morning. He still maintains he is innocent and I am still convinced the lad has a backup plan in place. If he didn't get Ronnie yesterday he has something else in mind for him. You tell Ronnie to take care and be ready for another go at him."

I replied, "He's already been warned of the likelihood of that happening and he has things in readiness for it. How about we organise a squaddie to get him home safely?"

"Nah, Ronnie will go to the View Road place and hold up there. It's an odd thing but they never go after civilians with these gang wars. Ronnie will stay at the gang place until this is all blown over. He won't risk his missus getting hit in any crossfire."

With that Bernie called me over for a second opinion on a commercial burglary. It looked like an inside job so she wanted a second opinion before she wasted any more police time. I reckoned it was an outside Job so she got the fingerprint lads involved and the photographer. Still it was good of her to get a second opinion when she was doubtful. I was getting to quite like having Bernie on our team. She bought a female perspective, if nothing else.

At 4.00pm I went back up to see Ronnie in his hospital bed. He was still adamant he had to take the attack on himself personally. As he explained it, "I have to do it for the sake of the patch if nothing else. I've already had a half dozen lads from around the country asking me if I need help on this one. Any member of the Mongrel mob has to take this personal. Think yourself lucky I haven't already got a dozen different gangs down here. There's no shortage of volunteers ready to sort Tohi and his mates out."

"Yeah, but then Tohi and his mates will have a half dozen of their gang members sitting on your patch as well. Your lads reckon you will be out of here tomorrow. Where are you going to go?"

"I'll hole up at View Road. The missus will be mad but I don't want her to get involved if anything does happen. Her and the kids will be safe enough at home if I am out of there."

"The Boss offered a squad car to take you home."

"He's a good lad but let's keep this all above the board. I'll have a motor ready for me and they have doubled the security on View Road. Just a reminder, Sarge, ring before you come and see me, the lads won't let just anyone in until we get this sorted. Oh and Sarge?"

"Yes, Ronnie"

"I'm still waiting on those grapes! Give your boss my best. I reckon you will be keeping him up to speed. I reckon he will be the one talking to Tohi. Tell Tohi that Ronnie sends his best wishes. I look forward to catching up with the guy. Cheers, Sarge."

With that I left Ronnie's bedside. I had a word with the two lads outside on guard and told them to stop chatting the nurses up. They also confirmed that Ronnie was doing his best to get out of the hospital tomorrow, I said I would be up to see Ronnie on the Monday and I would come to the Gang HQ to see him.

With that I went home and thought about what the weekend could bring. I had a golf game booked with the Boss and the Sarge and someone else on the Sunday. We had a rule that all cell phones must be turned off while we are having a game. Let's see if this one kept to the rules.

I got the call from Tim Cross just after 11.00pm. He said it looked like the other rapist, not the religious one. Did I want to get involved? I was already looking for my street clothes when he mentioned a rapist. I said I was ten minutes away. When he rang off I realised I was already in bed and in my pyjamas. So much for being free to do what you want when you grew up! It was only just 11.00 and I had been in bed for a half hour already!

I went up to Park Road and the reserve was readily evident. I parked up there along with the squad car and the ambo and Mike's car. The girl was being attended to in the ambulance so I had a word with Mike on the side of the street.

He said, "Be prepared for this one to be all over the place. She had been drinking. Reckons she's a virgin but she's 16 ½. The boyfriend is meeting us at the hospital and the girl should be there in a half hour."

"What do you mean 'all over the place.'"

Mike grinned, "The story is all over the place. Says she's a virgin and reckons she's spent the night at the pub drinking with her boyfriend. Those two don't always go together. I reckon you might need a WPC for this one."

I got on the phone to Bernie McDowell. She's the new detective and a senior constable. She'd know how to handle this. I told her to meet us at the hospital. She reckoned she would be there inside twenty minutes. I liked her attitude. She didn't waste time by asking stupid questions.

As I was talking on the phone to the new DC another car arrived. It was the father of the girl and he wanted to know what was going on. Once he was told loose details he wanted to go inside the ambo. Mike gently persuaded him he should leave the girl alone until she had spoken to us. From the father we also learned that mummy and daddy were none too happy with the boyfriend being on the dating scene. I suggested he go and pick up the mother and meet us down at the hospital.

I asked Mike to stay with the girl until she got to the hospital. By that time I would have the new DC on hand. That should be enough to keep all of the groups separated.

I got to the hospital and it sort of went downhill from there.

The girl maintained she was a virgin. Let's just say that the evidence was to the contrary and she looked like she enjoyed frequent relations with the boyfriend.

Mum and dad also thought she was a virgin so that was another conversation to be had with the boyfriend. The boyfriend was a year older than her so he wasn't breaking any laws other than that of shocking the father.

There was no DNA sample as the guy had worn a condom. There was however a couple of random pubic hair in among her hair. We hoped the boyfriend would not match that hair but that was for the DNA to sort out. Bernie did a great job in asking the girl questions and got a pretty straight forward set of answers to her questions. Let's say the girl and her boyfriend 'knew each other on regular occasions' and leave it at that.

Mother and father were distraught that their little innocent had been raped. The conversation with the boyfriend was something to be thought about much further down the line. The girl had to be asked if she might be pregnant as that could have an effect on her being given the morning after pill. When she assured the nurse she was not, only then could the pill be given. It might have been getting on for 1.30 in the morning when Bernie asked if she could slip away. She had to cover the Saturday shift and she needed her beauty sleep, she reckoned. I looked at my notes and said I would probably slip in for an hour and do the paperwork for the case.

Sunday

On Saturday nothing happened and I was always on alert of my phone to start ringing. I did go into the office and Bernie was out covering another call. I did my paperwork and went home. Not really a day off for me but Bernie was covering the Saturday shift and she was fairly efficient in dealing with anything that cropped up. I quite liked having a Senior Constable on the Squad. Bernie was suddenly the go-to-girl and she kept a lot of the questions from getting to me.

On Sunday I met up with the Boss and the Sarge and some guy named Thomas. I paired up with Thomas to make it an even match. It's odd how one person will beat the others for a week or so and then fall to the back of the leaderboard. That was the case with us three. For the last three weeks the Boss had won by a shot or two. Today he was all over the place and it was the Sarge's turn to win. He won by one stroke from me and the Boss was three strokes behind. Maybe it had something to do with the new handicaps. The Boss was down to a 28. I was nudging along with a 29 and the Sarge was struggling with a 31 handicap. But today it all worked out in the Sarge's favour as he sipped his celebratory beer.

It was only up in the clubrooms that we remembered to turn our phones back on. Then all hell broke loose. It seems that with us being out of contact the next senior person was the Chief Inspector! Some timid PC had been forced to ring the big Boss to ask for instructions as Bernie was out on a CIB enquiry concerning a domestic assault. It seems that there had been an attempt to take out Tohi. Tohi was on Te Ngae Road when a car tried to run him off the road. It had to be something to do with Ronnie. I don't believe in coincidences that much. Tohi also had some protection around him and the car driver had gunned his motor when Tohi's guards drew a weapon on the offending driver. The car sped up and turned off down Vaughans Road. It was fairly easy to get back to the right side of town from there. It might have been a half hour later that Ronnie had a motorbike come up behind him as he was driving to see his missus. The pursuing bike was all set to let a shotgun blast go from the pillion seat when the Ronnie's bodyguard caught up with the offender and they shot off up Clayton Road. The two bodyguards dithered until Ronnie caught up with them and they decided to keep Ronnie under wraps rather than chase the two Black Power members on the bike.

Now the upshot of all of this was that the CIB room fielded the call from Ronnie and the CI had to stop his golf game to attend to the incident with Tohi. Yes, there were other Squad cars on the scene but the CI was also in attendance. I don't quite know how he looked with his pringle sweater on but there was hell to pay on the Monday when the Boss was called upstairs to see the CI.

I went round to see Ronnie on my way back from my game of golf. He was at View Road and just a little pissed off that Tohi had made another attempt on him. When I mentioned the attempt on Tohi,

Ronnie grinned and made that 'innocent' face. I said I would be round to see Ronnie at 10 in the morning and I would want to go and see where the attempt on Ronnie had taken place.

<u>Monday</u>

On Monday morning the Sarge was only just in when he got the call for the Boss to go and see the big Boss. I was in at my usual time and it looked like it was going to be a stunning day. I had tossed up whether go dressed for cooler temperatures and the cooler temps had won. Now I was briefly regretting my choice of clothing. The Boss was down within twenty minutes of going upstairs. Obviously he and the big Boss had a few words but the Boss's attitude was that the lower minions (us) were not paid to be on duty 24/7 so if we wanted to turn our phones off we were entitled.

The big Boss knew he was on a loser but he did have a go at the Boss for turning his phone off. He didn't get that far as the Boss reckoned he wasn't paid enough to leave his phone on, either. They finally agreed to disagree and it would be 'imprudent' to turn our phones off when we had a situation brewing in our district. I think the Boss asked the big Boss how it felt to be back doing active police work for a change. At this point they might have had another discussion on relative pay rates. All I know is that my Boss was quite pleased with himself when he came back downstairs.

"Right." he said. "He who must be obeyed reckons it was rude of us lot to turn our phones off while we had a game of golf. I did mention that none of us were paid to work 24/7. He then had a go at me because he reckoned I made more than you lot. I told him the same answer. Then we had an appeal from he who must be obeyed to not turn our phones off when there is a possible situation developing." At this point the Boss used air quotes to indicate a 'possible situation developing'.

He continued, "If you are off duty I don't care whether your phones are on or off. It's your call. However if your phone is on there is always the chance you might get called in if a situation develops where we need all hands on deck. Right. Yesterday we had a possible attack on Ronnie and one on Tohi. Obviously both of them will deny being the instigator behind the attacks but I reckon we can call that one as a bit obvious. DS, you went to see Ronnie yesterday. Any comments?"

"I had a word with Ronnie. Yes, he denies everything about Tohi. I'm going up there to see Ronnie this morning and we're going to have a look at the scene of the attempted hit on Ronnie. Oh, yeah, Ronnie has leant to us his jacket for forensics. I should have something back on that today. I also have the lads from forensics going up to see Ronnie's bike today. Maybe we can get something from it. That's me, Boss."

The Boss took over the conversation again, "I went to see Tohi yesterday. He doesn't trust my Boss so he reckons he was pleased to see a friendly face. It seems that a car driver tried to nudge Tohi off the road yesterday. That was out on Te Ngae Road. Tohi reckons it was deliberate and it was only his two out riders that saved him from the driver. Driver zoomed off when Tohi's lads arrived. He shot off down Vaughans Road and the two riders stayed with Tohi. We can assume it might have been instigated by Ronnie. But that's about it. Right, what else have we got this lovely day, Sarge?"

The Sarge was quickly on to what had come over from the Squaddies. One commercial burglary, a couple of cases of GBH from Bernie yesterday, and there is a domestic assault that wants following up from Tim's night shift. All of this was taken on by Derek and Mike as Bernie was having a couple of days off due to working over the weekend.

The Boss quickly handed out assignments for the day and that left me to work with Ronnie, and the Boss to work with Tohi.

I started with taking the lads from the forensics lab up to Ronnie's. I had an interesting conversation with them as we drove round to View Road. When we got there to the gang HQ it was to be met with their full security. We had to wait outside until the vehicle that had been parked across the inside of the gate was pulled back. It was perhaps only for twenty seconds or so but it did remind me what my biggest problem was at that point.

Ronnie was there to greet us as the gates opened, "You fellers take a look at my bike and then we'll have a brew."

The forensics lads took a look at the bike and there seemed to be a lot of umming and aahing as their examination of the bike confirmed their thoughts. There was not a mark on the bike other than the scratches on the left hand side of the tank as Ronnie had dismounted the machine when it was still moving slowly. The scratches were from the bike being dropped and then hitting the ground or the pavement. Ronnie had adopted the use of 'Ape hangers' for his bike as he reckoned they were better for cruising and had little effect on the driver's fatigue levels. It was still fine to ride the vehicle away from the scene as it was only superficial damage. When the ambulance had arrived for Ronnie there were perhaps a dozen bikes on the scene. The ambo lads reckoned they were given star treatment as they attended to Ronnie's wound with a cordon around them, most of them with guns drawn. They also had an escort of four riders as they went back to the hospital to get Ronnie sorted out. The rest of the riders stayed at the scene as they tried to work out what had happened. They had found the place where the ambusher had lain in wait for Ronnie and they reckoned there were two lads waiting in hiding for Ronnie to drive by.

When we adjourned upstairs for a cuppa, the forensic lads told Ronnie he had been lucky to survive the incident. The forensics lads were thorough as they seldom got a chance to do any working out on a shooting victim. One of the lads, Paul Emery, was doing most of the talking as we had our cuppa.

"Yeah, our analysis of the jacket is confirmed by the state of the bike in that there were no bullet holes in the bike anywhere. You were hit in the left arm with a clean break of the left humerus. We also found a bullet crease mark on the right side sleeve, which would indicate to us that your right arm was being held slightly lower than the left. I'm going to guess that your arm was held lower because you were revving the machine up, possibly to go through the gears on your bike. I won't be able to tell whether you were going from second to third gear or third to fourth gear until we get to the site of the incident. I don't suppose you can recall, er Ronnie?"

"I've lived through the memory a few times since it happened. I'd reckon I was going from second to third. Is that important?"

I could imagine this forensics guy was in the habit of pushing his glasses up but the guy didn't wear glasses. Still it was important to him. "It's only important when we get to the site of the incident and try to determine the location from where the shots were fired."

Ronnie dismissed their query with, "Oh we've already found the spot. My lads had a look around after the ambulance left and they found it all right."

The forensics guy looked excited, "Don't tell me. I have a bet on it. It was about 1.5 meters above the street level. Perhaps 1.6 meters but not more than that. Am I right?"

"Yeah. About twenty meters from the road. One of my lads reckoned they would have been better off being about thirty or more meters back from the road, would have given them more of a lead time to get a steady shot away."

The forensics guy was happy he had been proved right. He went on, "Well that's what saved your life. Being that close to the road he had to have made a hurried shot. He was probably aiming for your central body mass, that's the heart area. Because he took a hurried shot, he led too far in front of you. How does it feel to know you were only a tenth of a second away from being dead?"

Ronnie was grinning," It certainly feels better being alive than dead. Was this guy an amateur? Maybe a hunter?"

The forensics guy was in his element, "Probably. You never get a target that close to you when you are out hunting, so you have to allow for a lead time. That's probably what saved your life."

Ronnie then turned to me, "Hey, Sarge. If I am out with you fellers, you got enough weapons to protect me? Or do I need to take a few of the lads with me."

"If it makes you feel safer you can take your lads with you. But I don't want to see any weapons you don't have licenses for. Okay?"

"Okay, Sarge. I'll tell them to keep them holstered." He was grinning at me. I returned the grin and we left the gang HQ. Ronnie got in my car and we drove up to the incident site, It was a quiet ride and I asked him how he felt, having just survived a shooting incident.

"Mortal, Sarge. Before I always reckoned I was somehow immortal being the boss of the gang. Now I'm grateful I have a wife and kids. I dunno. It's odd but I reckon life is fuller, or richer having someone you can talk about your day with."

I instantly thought about my own life. Was it empty? Not really. Would I be better having someone to talk to at the end of the day. Yeah, it was a possibility but I liked my lifestyle. Or had I just got used to it?

I was also concerned with Ronnie's health. He was obviously in pain but he didn't want to take any of the painkillers prescribed to him. He reckoned he didn't want to risk getting addicted to the pain killers. "That's a mugs game, right?" I think he was only taking a half dose of the painkillers he was on. To me that didn't seem too smart but then I had not been shot at recently.

We arrived at the scene of the crime and I parked fifty yards down the road. It had happened on Pukehangi Road. As you go up Sunset Road to the end and hang a right turn, there is a small left hand bend in the road. I could imagine Ronnie accelerating to second gear and then dropping to third gear as he rounded the bend and accelerating before dropping into fourth. He walked me and the forensic lads to the spot where he reckoned the attack had taken place. Then he walked me up to where he thought the gunman had hidden.

The forensics guy was doing his thing, "Yes, far too close to get a good shot away. And I reckon he would only be about 1.5 meters above the roadway. Yes, now if we take a look around..."

He wandered off to the right and then to the left of where the ambusher had waited then shouted, "And here it is."

He took out an evidence bag and bagged a shell cartridge for evidence.

"That's a fairly narrow window," he explained as he knelt down in the shooter's position. He confirmed with Ronnie the approximate site of the attack. "Er. Ronnie, can I have a couple of your chaps for a second or two."

The forensics guy then had two of Ronnie's lads go across the road and stand around twenty meters apart. Then he asked them to increase their distance to about twenty five meters. When he was happy he spoke to Ronnie, "I would really like the cartridge shell or the projectile. It should be within the range of those two lads standing on the other side of the road." We went across the road and found it within a few minutes of our search.

Again the bullet was bagged. Ronnie grinned and held the bag up," It doesn't have my name on it."

The forensics guy was happy. He had found the bullet in a tree about 1.2 meters above the ground.

"I can get on to this and I'll let you have the results by tonight. Hmm, I see there is still blood on the bullet. I assume that is Ronnie's er blood."

Ronnie asked for the bullet as a souvenir. I asked to hang on to it as evidence but I would let him have it after it was all over.

Now I had all of the evidence available I was somehow more satisfied.

I returned Ronnie to the Gang HQ and the forensics lads to their office and went back to the station where the Sarge was waiting for me.

The Boss had been having a word with Tohi. Tohi reckoned he would have to take the incident on Sunday as a personal attack from Ronnie. Evidently the Boss had had enough of the playing around. He might have said something that Tohi took offence to. For now, the Boss and Tohi were not on really good speaking terms. The Boss had then gone out to assist Derek with the case of GBH. The assailant had been rather verbal with his attack. The Boss was asked to go around and see if this guy needed calming down with a night in the cells. He spent the night in the cells. Not a good idea to start arguing with the Boss when he is in a bad mood!

That afternoon Ronnie went up to the hospital to get his wound dressed. It was good that the hospital realised the seriousness of having Ronnie wounded. He had been asked to go in for a checkup and then Ronnie had explained the situation he was in. The hospital were okay with Ronnie coming at short notice and leaving by the back door. It seems the hospital were also not keen on not having a gang war within their grounds either. For whatever reason they were doing it, I was pleased that Ronnie was being given a little leeway by the hospital.

I also got a call from the forensics lads. They were still working on Ronnie's bike and jacket but they did get a result from the pubic hair on the victim's crotch. It was a different person and they had asked the boyfriend to go and see them so they could eliminate him as the rapist.

That night I received a call from the rape victim. Although I did not have anything to report on she asked me if I would go and see her parents that evening. Her boyfriend was also coming round and I would be the one to keep everyone's tempers calm. I agreed to go round at 7.30 and try to diffuse the situation.

When I got there the father was surprised to see me until the girl victim said she had asked me to come along. The boyfriend was already there and tempers were starting to get frayed already. I sat there for an hour and I think I contributed to the conversation. When the father mentioned sexual relations I did ask if he had sexual relations when he was at that age. He reckoned it was certainly not for a lack of trying. When I turned it round and asked how he could be a hypocrite for his daughter not having sex at that age, I seemed to take away his whole argument. I left them chatting about protection and the like and not being too promiscuous. The father walked me to the door and shook my hand. He realised that rape was ever on the cards when his daughter was so well developed. Maybe he should have thought about it a bit more. I made a joke about not being able to lock up your daughters and he laughed. He did ask me to catch the bastard who had raped his daughter but I reckon he was more concerned with laying down a few ground rules for dating his daughter.

Chapter 3

T**uesday**

I didn't get the report from the forensics guy, Paul, until the next day. For whatever reason they were busy. The shell cartridge and the bullet both belonged to a Ruger 22, probably a magnum because of the bullet velocity and the lack of deflection. Evidently if the bullet has enough power behind it, it becomes harder for it to deflect. I really didn't understand the rest of the report, it got very technical. With the hospital report we had a probable match so that was all I was really interested in.

I had a sit down with the Boss, the Sarge and Derek and Mike. The key thing was that we were happy the situation had not escalated beyond our control. The Boss was trying to say that I should be the next one to talk to Tohi but I thought I had too good a relationship with Ronnie to jeopardise that. I also mentioned that the previous night I had been the referee between the rape victim and her parents. We agreed we had sod all on the rapist, not the religious one, and we agreed it was something we should also prioritize.

We talked about what we could expect to happen in the next few days. The Sarge reckoned we might have a few out of town gang members appearing in Rotorua. The problem I had is that I knew most of the lads in Ronnie's gang, new blokes I would not be able to identify easily so any new gang member could commit a crime and I wouldn't have a clue who he was.

We spoke for perhaps an hour before splitting up again. I had to update the file on Ronnie and the Boss had to update the file on Tohi. Things got a little awkward when the Boss had to ring the big Boss for the finer details on Ronnie's 'attempt' on Tohi. Things may have got a little heated between them until the Boss finished the call with 'Well give me a bloody pay rise and then I will keep my phone on!'

In the afternoon I went to see Janet. All that talk the previous day with Ronnie had made me a little lonely and the closest person I had was Janet. Yes, we did the thing, but I would have been quite happy enough to sit and have a chat with her. Well to be honest, yes' I was a bit lonely until she got naked and then all thoughts of being lonely went out of the window.

<u>Wednesday</u>

Another early summer day, although it was a little cold and not much chance of it warming up later on. Bernie was back on duty on the Wednesday. With her working Saturday and Sunday she took the Monday and Tuesday off. I took it upon myself to fill her in on what had gone on since her shift on Sunday. I did mention the Boss and the big Boss having a barney in the big Boss's office and then the Boss coming back downstairs to say he didn't care if people switched their phone on or off. We were entitled to our time off.

Bernie's only thought was that she was not in it with the big Boss for making him break off his golf game to attend the incident with Tohi. I told her not to worry. It was becoming quite a regular thing for the two of them to have a bust up in the big Boss's office. I said it cleared the air for a few days and then they would be civil with each other for a while.

I also got a call from the forensics lads. The boyfriend of the rape victim had a different DNA sample than the rapist. On the plus side we now had a sample of the rapists DNA. On the negative side we could only add it to the case file until we caught the lad in the act or something similar.

Seeing Bernie brought back Ronnie's conversation on Monday. How did one get a date at my age? With a decent bird? And what was I looking for in a bird? Good looking? Considerate? Sexy? Or was I looking for more of a Haus-frau type of thing. The solid woman who would look upon it as her duty to keep me fed and well, sexed... Maybe I should have a look at some of the dating sites and see what I had to choose from. With that small morsel in the back of my head for tonight I turned back to work thoughts. There were four calls from last night to attend to. I handed out the assignments to Derek and Mike and Bernie. I teamed up with Mike and we took two of the cases on. We had a GBH to tidy up from Tim Cross which involved us looking at the video from the Palace Tavern and a domestic burglary in the Malfroy Road area of town. The GBH was our first case. The Palace Tavern was open as the guys were cleaning up the place from last night. It was an obvious case of GBH and we took a copy of the video to give to the Crown Prosecutor along with the paperwork from Bernie.

Our domestic burglary was also an obvious case. Proof of forced entry through the kitchen window with obvious signs of the place being routed through as the burglars looked for something to steal. We got the fingerprint lads in to do their thing and Mike took some scene photos. It was one of those situations where we had no obvious villain so we would have to just wait and see if the burglars struck again and we might get them in the act or perhaps trying to sell off some of the stolen goods.

I got back to the Station and met up with the Boss, in his office.

The Boss was just saying it was too quiet for there to be a gang war when we got the call. One of Tohi's lads had been shot at over in Owhata. I should say that by now Owhata was to be thought of as Tohi's territory and the opposite side of town was Ronnie's patch. Where that left the middle of town was still open for further discussion or dispute.

One of Tohi's lads was cruising along Te Ngae Road when he felt a push alongside him. As he was traveling at around 70 KMH this was unusual. When he glanced down at his jacket he could feel some pain so he pulled over and stopped to take a better look. A bike roared past him and shot away.

Tohi's lad realised he had been hit so he got on his phone back to Tohi. Within a minute or two he was surrounded by his mates and ordered off to hospital. He had taken a shotgun blast across the lower right edge of his jacket. There was some penetration by the shotgun pellets and he had blood seeping out of his tee shirt. Fortunately his leather jacket had stopped most of the pellets. The ambulance arrived and he was treated initially at the scene and then he was placed in the ambulance and taken off to hospital. His bike was driven back to Gang HQ by one of his mates.

The Boss and I were in his car and on the scene before the ambulance arrived. There was a little unpleasantness as the other gang members took us as a personal affront to them but the Boss took it all in his stride. "Look, we can take a look at the scene of the crime or we can bugger off back to our nice warm office. Personally I don't really care. But I reckon you guys should make your bloody mind up and then let us get on with our job!" The Boss had a good way of speaking to the riders of the gang, and he was probably correct when he said he was just as happy going back to his nice warm office.

Just then Tohi arrived and he had a quick word with the Boss. Tohi then had a word with his gang members. "Listen. Leave the cops alone. They are neutral in this, let them give the scene the onceover. At least it's another gang looking for the bastards who did this."

Then Tohi turned back to the Boss, "Well, Detective Inspector, looks like she's all on now. Ronnie has made his move. Jimmy was just a new lad. He's only been patched for a week. His missus will be mad when I tell her."

Just then, a Holden Torna screeched to a halt behind the Boss's car and a woman got out crying and shrieking to high heaven. "Oh, hell. That's her now. Leave it with me and I'll sort her out." With that he went off to speak to the woman. The Boss got on the phone to get the print lads out and the Boss told me to take a few photos for the record. It's funny but as soon as I got my phone out and started taking images, the gang members decided to take a back seat and disappear.

The woman in the Torana shot off to the hospital. The fingerprint lads came and did their thing. There was some damage to the petrol tank of the bike which had caught the edge of the blast but it was fairly minor. By lunch time we were back in the office, eating our lunch and discussing the likely scenarios of what could happen now.

The Sarge reckoned Tohi would have to retaliate on one of Ronnie's lads. It was delegated to me to go and see Ronnie. I had to ask if Ronnie would give up his lads who tried to make the hit on Jimmy. Obviously I would be met with a 'no way'. But I had to go and see him anyway.

The Boss was pleased to see that Tohi was speaking to him again. It would make it easier for him to keep the lines of communication going with Tohi.

We had finished our lunch when we got the call that one of the visiting gang members had been the target of a retaliatory hit.

It seems that the visiting gang member had been minding his own business when he had been approached from behind while having a quiet beer. He had thought that the middle of town was a safe place to sit. He had been at the Checkers bar when he had been got at. Fortunately for him the back of the seat had taken most of the blast of the shotgun. He still had wounds from the blast but they were not as severe as might have been expected. He was wounded along his upper back where the chair had not covered him and also through the gap in the seat.

We shot round to the Checkers bar and surveyed the scene. The ambulance was already there and his wounds were not life threatening, fortunately. We appealed for any witnesses but no one came forward. Within a few moments there was a half dozen Mob members on site. No weapons were drawn but I could feel the tension in the air.

The ambulance left and the Boss and I tried to get anyone who had seen the incident to give us a description. It's funny but when gang members are involved, then no one else wants to get involved.

The newspapers had not covered the initial shooting as a gang war. It was initially reported as minor incident where a hunter had been too close to the road when he was out hunting. That may have something to do with the way it was reported from the big Boss. I doubted whether that would last for long, though.

I went up to the hospital in the Boss's car and he made sure to leave the 'Police Business' sticker on the front of the Boss's motor. That reminded me to ask how he had got the sticker in the first place.

I wound my way to the A&E dept and interviewed the victim. Fortunately, there was one of Ronnie's lads there who vouched for me to the victim. Once I was vouched for, the victim opened up.

"Nah, never heard a thing. last thing I remember was having a quiet beer and checking out the birds. Then I wake up in the ambulance and I am up here. I reckon those buggers would have got me from close range though. I have a hell of a headache now. I reckon that was from the noise of the shotgun And I only had one beer."

To say I got nothing from the victim would be an understatement. As far as he was concerned it was the price of being a mob member, the occasional time when someone walks up behind you and blasts you with a shotgun. I find it difficult to live with that mentality. For me I want to live to see the end of the day.

I spent a half hour with him until he was taken away for surgery to remove the pellets from his back. Then I went back to the Checkers bar but the Boss had already walked back to the station. When I got back I reported on the victim although there was very little to report.

The Sarge did say that we knew how Ronnie would take the hit on his man. What we didn't know was what would happen next.

That night I went online for dating apps. That is how the world works today. Did you know there are even apps that are strictly for the gay guys. It's called Grinder if you don't believe me. I assumed there were now also apps for cross gender and trans sex people but I did not pursue my enquiries further in that direction.

I focused on Tinder because I had heard of that one. Even Tinder offered me the chance to be very adventurous in my search. I won't say any more about that but Tinder does cater to all tastes.

I filled in the online form and I was met straight away with over a hundred matches. Just for a laugh I responded to a few. That was a mistake! I kept getting response from girls who wanted to be naughty and be taught a lesson from someone who purported to be a policeman. One even sent me a picture with a place where I could insert my truncheon. It was a graphic photo! We don't even have truncheons nowadays, and if I was put in that position I haven't a clue what I would do.

I switched the site off as I was just a little repulsed by some of the replies I was getting. I went back to watching You Tube to see how people of my age got dates, nowadays. Unfortunately Tinder came up as the leading site but evidently I had to be careful with what I put on my search. Oh, and never use your real name. I did get that from one of the sites I visited with. Too late for me!

On the Wednesday night I got a call from the rape victim's father. I could tell him we had a match for the pubic hair as the rapist but other than we had nothing. After his call I also rang the other two victims to give them an update of what we had so far. Okay, it wasn't much but it did show we were still involved in looking for the rapist.

Thursday

A nice day for a change. Well, weather wise that is.

I was in just before 8am and the Sarge already had my coffee ready for me. The Boss almost followed me in so we sat down to talk about what we could expect next.

The Sarge was optimistic, "The last time we had a gang war we would have a period of three or four days where we wouldn't have anything happen. Yesterday was retaliation for both sides. It wouldn't surprise me if we have a quiet spell for a day or two. Then we might get something better planned to deal with. Going up to someone who is sat outside a pub having a beer and blasting him with a shotgun is amateur stuff. I reckon both Ronnie and Tohi are capable of better planning than that. However we don't know when they will strike so we have to be ready for the buggers whenever they decide to have a go."

I have to be honest and say that waiting for them to plan something was the better option so we didn't have dead bodies on the street. But on the flip side waiting for them to come up with a foolproof plan didn't thrill me, either. That also meant dead bodies for us to sort out.

The cases from the squad room were handed out to the lads. That's another thing I have to stop saying. We have a female on our team now. The lads and Bernie received the cases from the Squad room. I was expected to go and see Ronnie and hope we could get something out of him. The Boss was set to go and see Tohi on a similar futile quest.

Among the items for discussion were whether we should have our regular golf game on Sunday. The Boss reckoned we should not let the gangs tell us when to have time off so the Sarge rang and organised it.

I went to see Ronnie after phoning him first. He was always pleased to see me and we sat and had a chat for a half hour. I was introduced to a few of the lads that were visiting for a few days. They thought they would take in Rotorua and see what it had to offer them. It all sounded very casual if you didn't know there was a gang war brewing! Ronnie seemed to be coping with the pain of his injury a bit better. I didn't ask if he was taking the pain medication as it would seem a bit of weakness with him. On reflection, I should have asked!

I returned to the station and sat down with the Sarge and the Boss in the centre of the office.

Just then the Boss's phone rang. It was the big Boss!

The local newspaper had finally caught up with the story. We were now being entertained with stories of a gang war brewing in Rotorua.

They had photos of the shooting at the pub yesterday. They had a photo of the ambulance leaving as 'they rushed the innocent victim to the hospital for life saving surgery'. As far as I was aware he didn't actually need lifesaving surgery and as for the innocent victim side of the story, well you know my views on that!

The big Boss was looking for an angle on the story that might paint the police in a better light. The Boss had picked up the call on the phone on my desk so we had a clear understanding of what was being said.

"There's a story about a gang war in town."

The Boss looked a bit surprised, "Possibly because there is a gang war in our fair city. I reckon the shooting at Checkers might have given the local rag a bit of a heads up on that," replied the Boss.

"Yes I had worked that out for myself. What are we going to do about it?"

"It's the same with any gang war. We wait for them to act and then we do what we can?"

"We should be going and seeing these lads. Both sides of them. Maybe we can head them off before it gets too bad."

The Boss was getting just a touch sarcastic with his responses to the big Boss." I've been to see Tohi four times this week and the DS has been to see Ronnie the same amount. What do you reckon? Should we move in with them?"

"Don't be sarcastic with me, DI. Is there anything else we could do to broker a peace?"

"We've done everything we can in terms of meeting with them. After that it's just a case of waiting to see what they get up to and react accordingly."

"Hang on. I have Division on the other line. I'll call you back later."

With that the big Boss hung up and my Boss returned to the conversation he was having with us. "It appears that he is getting a call from Divisional HQ. Maybe it made the nationals. Sarge, pull up the local rag and see what they have said."

The Sarge pulled up the site of the Daily Post and we all looked at what it said. They really had nothing to work with. There was a lot of 'sources close to the...' and a bit more of 'an undisclosed source has reported' but they had nothing concrete to work with. It was all supposition and a photo of the chair the guy was sitting on when he was shot. They also had a close up of the chair showing the damage to the chair. Yeah, they were struggling to get a story together. We looked at the story in some detail but there was not a lot of interest to us.

The Sarge turned the site off and we sat and had a few more minutes discussing the story. Then we decided what we could do to minimize the gang war. We knew we had to wait for the individual gangs to do something and then we would react to it. Personally I hated being in that position.

The Sarge reckoned we should get into the habit of going up to the gang's HQ at least once a day. If they were expecting us they would know not to do anything on their home turf. The Boss agreed.

We had nothing more to go on so we had a cuppa and then we went out to see the gang leaders.

I went to see Ronnie and the Boss went to see Tohi.

As always, I rang first before my visit. Ronnie said it was OK so I headed up to View Road.

Ronnie greeted me as I walked through the front gates of his gang HQ. I noticed there was a district nurse attending Ronnie as we spoke. She was a no nonsense kind of girl and she was talking to Ronnie as I was also taking to him. She finished up and left as we continued talking. Ronnie said, "Thanks. Maggie." as she left.

"Good to see you Sarge. It must be at least a day since I last saw you." Ronnie was in a good mood. I still declined to mention the pain killers he was on. Instead I took the opportunity to ask him about his defenses.

"Take a look around, Sarge. I reckon you are on our side so feel free to take a look." I didn't correct Ronnie that I was really on nobody's side but I did take a look at his set up. I went downstairs and wandered around the site. I was impressed.

The place was like a fortress. The walls were about three meters or three and a half meters high. All of the fence supports were set in concrete which came out about a meter out of the ground and there was strong razor wire set between the posts. On top there was a platform so that the defenders could hide behind a wall and it looked like there was some form of ply around the interior edge of the wall. It looked like it was at least a couple of centimeters thick. If any gang wanted to assault this place they would have to be well armed. Across the gates was a car that looked like it was there to prevent another vehicle being used as a battering ram to gain access. I was impressed at his set up and said so when we were walking upstairs for our regular cuppa. He reckoned he had inherited it from the last leader of the gang but it was adequate. He then asked if I wanted to take a look at his armory. Maybe Ronnie was a little high from the drugs he was on, but I couldn't miss this chance.

He took me into his armory. He had twice as much weaponry as the local law did. I didn't really take it all in but he would have had 50 or more shotguns, the same or a higher number of rifles and at least that many pistols. Ronnie then sat me down for a cuppa.

"Maybe I shouldn't have showed you the armory but at least you know we are well prepared for a defence of our place if we are pushed. And, don't forget, Sarge, nearly all of our lads are armed as they go round town. So you can add that to what you just seen in the armory."

"And you reckon all of those are legal?"

"Legal, schmeagle. I'd say most of them are paid for. Does that count?" He giggled at his mirth.

"Thanks, Ronnie, for trusting me. I'm not going to get the AOS lads out here to do a tally. If you say they are legal that's ok with me."

Was it my imagination or was Ronnie just a bit high?

"Ronnie how are you doing with the medications? The prescriptions you are on?"

Ronnie sobered for a second. This was not a good sign as I had seen a few druggies in my time. They can flash into a different reality in the blink of an eye.

"I've been better, Sarge. Now I just have to cope with this." He lifted his left arm, or he at least tried to. "You're right, Sarge, I got to get off of these drugs."

With that he seemed to slump into a snooze. The effort of lifting his arm had caused him some grief and he had slipped into a doze. Maybe it was a sleep thing? His guards lifted him into a comfy chair. I had a word with the two guards.

"Is he often like this?"

"Just the last few days. He might have been mixing his meds. He might be having a bit of weed when it gets too much."

"And you're letting him make the decisions in a bloody gang war!"

"He's the boss!"

"Well don't let him decide anything important if he is as high as a bloody kite."

With that I left the gang HQ and went back to the station. I reported into the Boss who then called the Sarge in and made me repeat myself.

"Ronnie is as high as a kite. He's supposed to be making decisions and he is spaced out. He had a doze before he could get to finish speaking with me. The gang reckons he is the boss so he makes the decisions and they will do what he wants. It's not good at the Mongrel mob!"

The Boss spoke up, "I have just got back from Tohi's place in Vaughans Road. He's planning something but I can't get him to tell me what they are planning. I don't know what it is but it will be a biggie and it will be against Ronnie."

I had noticed a few new gang members on the streets of Rotorua in the last day or so and I mentioned this to the Sarge and the Boss. Just then we were joined by Bernie and Mike. The Boss invited them to sit with us and the chat continued.

Mike had also noticed a few new members of both gangs being in town. It was either new recruits or gang lads from out of town gangs looking to reinforce the locals.

The Sarge reckoned they were still about even in numbers so we shouldn't expect anything from them until one of them had reached a position of superiority in numbers or else had developed a huge tactical advantage. Ronnie deciding to do things when he was high could be considered a tactical advantage for the Black Power. The Boss looked a little shocked but the Sarge was adamant. "It's not often I insist but I reckon I am right. If Tohi learns about Ronnie being high we could have a major escalation in activity."

I was listening and learning from the Sarge and the Boss's experience. Reluctantly the Boss agreed and that got me worried.

The rest of the day passed uneventfully. I busied myself on small stuff that had not garnered my attention the first time I had come across it - Divisional memos about someone being promoted. That type of thing. I managed to make it to five o'clock and went home to make myself some tea.

During the early evening I went on Tinder. Let me say I was astounded at how many responses I had about my ad the previous evening. First I got rid of all of the girls who wanted to make contact from overseas. If they looked that good in a photo, why were they not already set up with a bloke?

Then I got rid of anyone who lived more than 100 kilometers from me. I had asked for only local ladies to respond. Then, thanks to my knowledge of the local crims I got rid of anyone who had a criminal record. Let's be honest, if they sounded a bit dodgy they were also dumped as well. I was still left with 28 people within 100 kilometers from me! By the time I whittled the list down I still had a dozen to pick from. Maybe this tinder thing was not so bad after all.

I PMed one of the ladies who had replied and arranged to have a coffee with her on the Saturday. She was from Rotorua so I arranged to meet her at Capers for a coffee and a chat. With that I went to bed and had a pleasant night.

Friday

And it was another glorious day. Weather anticipated to get into the low twenties. With this kind of weather I knew it would be a good day. Friday seemed to be a favoured night for the rapist so I half expected to get a call once I had hit the land of nod!

Getting into the office I came close to beating the Sarge in but he had just put the coffee pot on, or whatever it is that you call these things. It seems a bit odd to call it a pod machine. That conjured up images of Doctor Who and the Tardis.

I settled down for my coffee with the Sarge. I suppose it was because it was on my mind that I mentioned going on Tinder to the Sarge. He reckoned I was mad for going onto something that was so trendy. He didn't exactly say that it was mad 'for someone of my age' to go on Tinder, but the inference was there. I reckoned I would be getting invites to come and have dinner with the Sarge and his wife, Huia, as they tried to set me up with one of Huia's mates. But that was in the future. On Saturday I had a coffee planned with one of the Tinder ladies. The Boss walked in and just as the Sarge was about to say something about Tinder I said I would prefer to keep it between us so he thought better of it.

With our coffee over, the Boss asked if anything had come over from the squad room or from Tim that he wanted a follow up on. There were four cases from the squad room so the Boss allocated them out to the rest of the lads, I have to stop saying that. We have a bird on our team, now. The Boss and the Sarge and I sat down for a talk in the Boss's Office.

The Boss started, "Right I've been thinking about the problem you have with Ronnie."

Suddenly it was my problem?

"We can't let Ronnie be making decisions when he is high on drugs. I reckon we should be seeing him at least twice a day until we can rely on his judgement, again."

I agreed but also said we can't make decisions for him. The Boss reckoned it might be splitting hairs as to whether we were making decisions or whether Ronnie was doing the decisions but with our guidance.

I did ask why we were concerned about Ronnie's decisions but the Sarge intervened and said we were better with the devil we know, as in Ronnie being in charge, than some other lad who came through the ranks and might be a fierier character and then we end up with all out gang warfare in our streets.

I could see the Sarge's point but I didn't really want to get involved in one side of a gang war. I had nothing to do so I rang Ronnie. He didn't answer the phone but of his offsiders did and suggested I come up for a coffee. I should have known this was a bad sign as Ronnie and I always had a cup of tea.

I went up to the gang HQ and waited to be identified and the car inside to be pulled back so I could enter. Ronnie was nowhere to be seen so I went upstairs and into the kitchen where we usually had our cuppa.

Ronnie was inside but it was obvious he was high. He greeted me as if he was expecting me and one of the underlings made us a brew. Normally Ronnie would have made us a brew. If his own gang members were reluctant to even trust him with a jug, that was not a good sign.

We sat down and Ronnie was there but he was also not there. I had to literally snap my fingers to make him realise I was talking to him. Once I had his attention he was not too bad but I could see he was high.

I spoke to one of the underlings who was also one of his lieutenants and made an excuse to speak to him on some other matter. When I managed to get him on one side the conversation was not that good. "Ronnie is high as a bloody kite. You can't let him make decisions about the gang when he is in this state."

"He is the boss!"

"Well you can tell him that when you are all members of the Black Power mob!"

"What can we do? Like I said he is the boss!"

"Is there another gang leader we can trust. What about one of you taking over for a while?"

"Tananga is down from Auckland. Maybe he could have a word with Ronnie. He's one of the Bosses of the Auckland Mob. As for anyone else taking over, no thanks. With the mood he is in anyone offering to take on the leadership would be seen as trying to get him out. That's a quick way to find yourself out in the wop-wops with a bullet in your brain."

"Okay. So who is this Tananga and where do I find him?"

"He'll be in in an hour, he usually is. He's a bit worried about Ronnie but Ronnie is the boss so whatever he says goes."

I said I would be back in an hour and went back to the Station.

First I rang Mike from the morgue to get the name of a Doctor I could speak to.

Next I rang Richard Newberry who was the doctor Mike had recommended.

I had a good chat with Richard. I described the symptoms of Ronnies apparent high and he knew I immediately what was happening.

"it sounds like your mate is mixing his meds. He is on a high strength of, well it's a morphine based drug and he will probably need it for at least another few days, if I am reading his chart right. It sounds like he is mixing it with, I'm going to say Wacky Baccy. Does he sell that? Because if he does, he will be taking inordinately high amounts of Wacky Baccy to try and keep himself on a level. The morphine does tend to induce an artificial reality and I've seen it before where they take cannabis to try and get some control back in their life. Usually it's a bad idea and they end up being dependent on the morphine and the cannabis to get through their day."

I interrupted, "So how long will he need to take the morphine stuff?"

"Probably another five days or more," Richard replied. "It's not a clean break where the bone will knit neatly. We had to put a plate in to get the bone to replace itself. He will probably always have a weaker arm on the left. It's mixing the morphine and the cannabis that will do the damage. He could end up dependent on both. If you want my advice, tell him to knock off the cannabis. It will be hard enough to knock off the morphine if he is not mentally strong."

I thanked Richard for his advice and sat and thought about the situation for a while. Before long it was time to head back to the gang HQ and see Tananga, the boss of the Auckland Mob.

I rang again and was told it was fine for me to come and see Ronnie. Also Tananga was also there if I wanted to speak with him.

I made my way back to View Road and waited for a few seconds for the car to be pulled from across the inside gateway.

Once inside I was met with Ronnie. He had forgotten I had already been there an hour or so prior and he greeted me like a long lost friend. "Sarge. Good to see you. Wanna brew?"

Ronnie was spaced out again. This was not a good sign. I said I would like to see Tananga for a few moments. Ronnie was immediately just a touch suspicious. It's not unusual for druggies to be instantly suspicious. In fact it's usually a sign they are doing drugs when they get instantly suspicious about your motives. I told Ronnie I wanted to see how Auckland gang life was and who better to ask than Tananga.

At that Ronnie agreed it was a great idea and said he would delay putting the jug on until I had my chat with Tananga.

I was introduced to Tananga and Ronnie was called away to make some decision.

Tananga was a reasonable guy to speak to. He said he was disappointed to see Ronnie was puffing away on cannabis while he was also on the drugs from the hospital. He was sufficiently disappointed to think about heading home and picking up the pieces of what was left of the Rotorua Chapter when it was all over.

I explained what Richard, the Doctor, had told me. I explained about the difficulty of getting away from the morphine habit and said it would be ten times more difficult if Ronnie was also using cannabis.

Tananga knew what I was asking for. "So you lads want me to assist Ronnie with his decisions until he gets clean again."

I replied, "I don't want a gang war on our streets."

Tananga said, "I'll hang around for a while but it's only for a fellow Mob member. It's got nothing to do with helping the bloody Police out. Gottit?"

With that we went and had a brew with Ronnie. Now that Tananga could get closer to Ronnie, he could see how bad he actually was. Somehow the subject of staying off the wacky baccy was raised and although Ronnie reckoned he had it under control, I could see Tananga was already formulating a plan.

My work was done, for the moment, and I told Tananga that I would probably drop in on the odd occasion to see how he was. Tananga reckoned I had better be dropping in every day to check on Ronnie or there could be problems. Whatever happened, I could now see some hope for the next week or so.

I went back to the Station and told the Sarge and the Boss what had happened with Tananga. The Boss reported back from his visit with Tohi. The Boss had the opinion that Tohi was still planning something but he could not get a feel for what it was.

That afternoon I had arranged for the team to go out to the clay pigeon range out by the dump. I wanted them to be familiar with all types of weapons, so I had arranged this as something of a novelty for them. We were guided by a few of the local members and I was pleasantly surprised to see the half a dozen shotguns we had to play with were all of a superior grade. I had a Smith & Wesson to play with which was very nicely balanced. I had the team learn about the various bore reducing methods which meant the spread pattern of the Shotgun pellets was increased or reduced whichever one you chose. Then, once we had the safety talk, we were all allowed to use the shotguns on a load of 25 clay pigeons. The Sarge and I drew equal first with 18 out of 25 hits. When we had a shoot off, the Sarge won with 17 hits to my 16. Then we adjourned to the Clubroom and had a beer or two. I was quite getting into my role as the CIB instructor and doing something like this was a change for the lads and Bernie. The Boss was not quite so fortunate with his turn at the shooting. He only got 12 of the 25 and came equal last with Derek. Still I had the team out playing with some top quality shotguns for a change. Interestingly the shotguns were only good for a range of perhaps 25 to 50 meters and then they quickly lost effectiveness as the pellets began to slow down. Maximum range of a shotgun was less than 200 meters as by that range the pellets had lost all of their oomph. In fact, as I understood it by the time the pellets his 200 meters they would all be on the ground!

I got home at 6.00pm and made myself a brew. I sat outside on the lawn and enjoyed it. I had put in a good days work today.

<u>Saturday.</u>

I was right on time for my coffee appointment. I hesitated to call it a date as we were just meeting for a coffee. I parked up the road and went into Capers at precisely the right time. She was already there and she was wearing the apricot Jumper as she said she would.

I ordered the coffees and I also paid for them. That might have been an error as I should have checked she wasn't into paying for her own coffee. I have to say that nowadays with all of this gender equality and women's lib I really don't know who pays for what. To say I was already a little out of my depth was an understatement.

Fortunately, Pauline was great. We both knew straight away that we were not really meant for each other. In a way it was a blessing as we could then relax and enjoy just having a coffee with a new friend.

Pauline had been on the dating scene for a while. Occasionally she met someone and they might see each other a few times before one of them got bored. Occasionally sex would be involved but it would only be for the fun of it and nothing like a serious relationship. She gave me the heads up about dating for middle aged people. Tinder was the way to go and the App to use. There were others but Tinder seemed to take notice of reviews and if you misbehaved you could be kicked off the Tinder App. I was introduced to the world of custody. It did depend on which partner had custody of the shared kids and whether the parent could make it out for a date that weekend. All of this was totally new to me. We also talked about the etiquette of expecting sex after a date. Unless the partner was strongly indicating sex was on the table you should not expect it from your partner. It might be three or four dates before sex was on offer. If it got to more than four times without sex then that person was probably not into sex and you could give him or her the flick. If that was your intent, obviously.

I was fascinated at all of this new info, for me, and I offered to buy her lunch if she was going to continue giving me the heads up. She laughed and said she would pay for her own lunch but she was quite happy to talk for a little while longer.

I learned a lot from Pauline. I was at the point of taking notes when I realised I was not at work and it would be impolite. She left at close to 2.00pm and gave me a peck on the cheek as she was leaving. She had enjoyed meeting a total newbie to dating and it gave her the chance to tell me not to make the mistakes she had made when she was first dating. I did ask her about the subject of sex, as in how did I know it was on the cards. She laughed and then gave me a few suggestions I would never have even thought of. In terms of who does what and when the guy should take charge etc. She was refreshingly frank and it seems that it's not only the guys who enjoy sex. Nowadays it's something of a participation sport.

After Pauline left I went home and arranged to meet one of the other ladies on Tinder for a drink on the Sunday evening.

Then I remembered I was supposed to go and see Ronnie and Tananga so I shot up there for a half hour. Ronnie looked in pain so I had a word with Tananga.

"I had a word with him yesterday. I told him to lay off the weed while he was on the other pills. This is his first day away. It will be hard but I've told all of his own mob to not give him anything unless they get past me first. It's for his own good. Ronnie's a great lad and he has a good rep among the gangs. I'll get him through this."

I thanked Tananga and left. Ronnie asked me for a smoke until he remembered I didn't smoke and then he shut up. I was sad to see Ronnie so vulnerable. Hopefully it would make him stronger on the other side when he recovered.

Sunday

I met up with the Boss and the Sarge for my game at Springfield. I won by one shot from the Boss and the Sarge was distant three shots behind. I enjoyed having a beer on the Sarge as it was not often he ended up paying for the beers on a Sunday.

On the Sunday evening I met with Anne at the Belgian Bar for a beer.

Anne was definitely different. For a start she wouldn't shut up! She kept up 90% of the talking and it was all I could do to get a word in edgeways. She was very nice but very nervous. When I suggested I drop her off at home she seemed resigned that she would have to put up with more sex from a bloke she had only just met. I assured her that I wasn't expecting any nooky from the evening and she seemed pleased. A little surprised but still pleased. I put her down as probably not someone to drink with again and dropped her off. I didn't even give her a kiss as she left the car. She was probably of the opinion that I did not find her attractive. I thought she was very attractive but not the type of bird I was looking for so I didn't want to build her hopes up.

<u>Monday</u>

On Monday when I got into the station, the Boss was already in and the Sarge was making my coffee. I sat down in the Boss's Office and the Boss said, "Well?"

"Well, What?"

"You met up with the bird on Saturday. How did it go?"

I turned and looked at the Sarge as if to say, 'that was supposed to be private!'

The Sarge returned my look with an expression that said, "Well, I couldn't not tell the Boss about something this juicy."

I sort of wanted to tell them but I realised I actually had sod all to say. I had been out with a couple of Tinder ladies and had not got past any milestones or bases. I simply said, "A Gentleman does not tell tales about his love life."

My taking of the high road was met with, "That means he didn't score."

My farther protestations were met with. "Probably didn't even get past first base, either."

At that point Mike and Derek walked in so I was spared any further embarrassment. The conversation turned around to the gang war.

I reported to the group about Ronnie and his progress and the fact that Tananga was calling the shots at the Mongrel Mob. The Boss reckoned I had made a smart move until we had learned about how Tananga liked to deal with issues.

The Boss made some comment about Tinder. I was horrified. He then went on to say that the atmosphere in town was like Tinder. And it would only take one spark to set it alight. I knew he was having a dig at me and my reticence to speak details but I think he might have gotten away with it.

The Sarge handed out four cases from the weekend from across at the Squad room. Derek and Mike handled those cases. They were now becoming a useful asset to the CIB team along with Tim and Bernie. So I could do my thing with Ronnie with some comfort. The Boss went off to see Tohi and I went to see Ronnie after ringing first.

Ronnie was not great, but he had realised in his more lucid moments that he was on a slippery slope mixing the morphine with the cannabis, so he was quite determined to succeed. He also had his extended family to deal with and take care of. That would be his beloved Mongrel Mob. Civilians were going round to Ronnie's house and checking on his missus and the kids so he had not a lot to do other than concentrate on getting better. He only had a couple of more days on the morphine pills and he was determined to go cold turkey once they had finished.

Tananga took me on one side and said he was hearing reports of a protection mob going around town, starting on the east side of town on Amohau St. I'd have called it the South side of town but that was by the by. He had heard that if you paid $100 a week your shop would have no damage done to it in the event of a gang war. He asked my opinion on what he should do. I didn't have an answer for him. The obvious choice of who was doing this would be Tohi and his gang. Also obvious was that Tananga would have to do something starting on their side of town and quickly!

Once Tohi had a foothold on the town that would leave the Mob just their own patch on View Road to protect. Also, blindingly obvious to me, was that I could not advise Tananga to set up their own protection squad and seal off their half of town. I was still a copper!

I took the matter under advisement and promised to get back to Tananga once I had consulted with the Boss. I then hightailed it back to the office to consult with the Boss and/or the Sarge if the Boss was not available.

Fortunately the Boss had returned from seeing Tohi and was not in a great mood. We convened in the Boss's office. "He's still planning something and I can't get it out of him what he is planning. He just nods and looks smug."

I could answer the Boss's enquiry and I did, "Your mate Tohi is going around offering protection to the shopkeepers in town. For $100 a week their place won't get damaged if it hits the fan. The way they are talking, it's when it hits the fan rather than if!"

"The Sarge was thinking out loud, "But if the shops do get damaged, what happens then?"

"I dunno. Maybe they give them the $100 back!"

The Sarge was about to say something to the effect that I should not bite his head off when he was only thinking out loud, when the Boss chipped in. "That's what the bastard is doing. He's offering protection, the money doesn't matter. But if he is offering protection that means they won't start a fight in the protected areas. How is Ronnie taking the news?"

"That's what I have come to talk to you about. Ronnie, rather Tananga, has asked me what he should do. I can't necessarily tell him he should do the same starting on his side of town."

"Oh, hell" was the summary response to my entreaties. I sat and watched as the two greatest thinkers in my life came up with nothing!

"You could always.... Maybe not" was the Boss's best shot.

The Sarge bettered it with, "What we need to do is... oh we can't do that because we are the law!"

The Boss came up with a decision, "We should go up through the Boss and ask Division. Perhaps see if they have come up with anything like this."

I'd had enough, "And we should have a response in maybe two or three weeks? I need an answer now!"

The Boss walked over and shut his office door. "You tell this Tananga lad to do whatever he thinks is best for the Mob. We can't have Tohi running around like he owns the place. Try to make it sound like you are not official."

"And how do I do that?"

And the Boss raised his voice to me, "Just bloody do it and don't tell me about it!" With that he ushered the Sarge and I out of his office and got on the phone.

"What do you reckon?" I asked the Sarge.

"Unofficially do what he says. At least if this Tananga lad gets on to it smartly we will still have a fairly even division of town. You do remember what I said last week about the town being divided down the middle. I hate to say it, but it looks like I was right."

Chapter 4

I went up to see Ronnie and Tananga. I was in something of a quandary. My gut instinct was to tell Tananga he had better get onto sewing up his side of town with a protection squad, just to keep the town reasonably divided and fairly equal. On the other hand I could not participate in anything that looked like I was favoring one gang over another. Neither could I go against my job as a policeman by saying I recommended he go and try to protect the other half of town so he could maintain some territory.

I sat down with Ronnie and Tananga at the gang HQ. I thought it might be best for them to ask me questions so waited for that time.

Tananga, "So what do you reckon, Sarge? I should go and do what Tohi is doing."

I replied. "Tananga, Ronnie, I cannot condone, as a sworn officer of new Zealand Police, that you commit to that action."

Tananga spoke again, "So what do you reckon we should do?"

I said it again, "Tananga, Ronnie, I cannot condone, as a sworn officer of new Zealand Police, that you commit to that course of action."

Tananga said it again, "So what does that leave us to do?"

Fortunately Ronnie got the gist of what I was trying to say. "Tane, he's saying he can't say that as a copper but he is telling you to go ahead and bloody do it!"

"That's not exactly what I am saying, but if I wasn't a copper, that's what I would be saying!"

At last Tananga understood what I was trying not to say. I reckon the Boss might have been pleased with how I handled it. I turned my attention to Ronnie, "Ronnie how are you doing? How is the arm?"

"It's bloody painful, Sarge but I'm taking on board about not mixing the pills and the weed, so I have to put up with it."

"Hang on let me give the pill pusher a ring."

I rang Richard Newberry the Doctor I had spoken to on Friday. I explained the situation to him without mentioning any names. He already knew the situation I was in because he was a regular reader of the Daily Post. He appreciated the discretion of the situation. He suggested I come in and get some half strength pills so that when Ronnie was being weaned off the full strength pills he would not be tempted to go back on the cannabis. He suggested Ronnie go on the half strength pills for another week. By that time he should be in way less pain and be able to just take paracetamol or something similar. Richard was a good guy and he knew the situation I found myself in. He would ask the Doctor who treated Ronnie to send out a prescription for the half strength pills and I could collect them from the Urgent Pharmacy.

I got off the phone to Richard and told Ronnie what I had organised. He was grateful. I think Tananga was a little surprised at how different we were to the Big City coppers, but he didn't say anything.

While I was on the subject I also suggested that Tananga and any of the lads to not visit any of Shi Low's people. They had their own protection thing going and it was not burdened by the laws of New Zealand when it came to dealing out retribution. He agreed to be careful so I gave him the names of any businesses that involved Shi Low's countrymen.

Tuesday

In at my usual time I was met with a coffee by the Sarge. I hadn't gone back to the station the previous day so the Sarge wanted an update on any developments. I was telling the news when the Boss walked in so I stopped and started again.

I told them about Tananga and what I had arranged with the Doctor who treated Ronnie. The Boss asked me how I had handled the situation of speaking to Ronnie about protection. I told him how I had handled it and he reckoned I had handled it well. I considered that a plus for me in the diplomacy stakes. The Boss had been to see Tohi again and still had nothing concrete to work with. Fortunately I had already told him about the protection set up by Tohi and now by Ronnie and Tananga. So he was pleased. I said I would go and see Ronnie later in the day so it was only down to the Sarge to hand out the cases from the Squad room. I ended up with a domestic assault because I had dealt with the earlier complaint by the same woman. Derek and Mike took on the rest of the cases. I also mentioned I had expected to hear about another sex assault by the rapist but we had heard nothing. The Sarge reckoned it wasn't unusual for them to go quiet for a while.

I was finished within a half hour on the domestic assault. She still declined to press any charges against the hubby so I told her there was nothing I could actually do for her. That may have been something of a white lie as I was still wrapped up in the gang war situation. She promised to ring me if it ever happened again.

I went up to see Ronnie but I forgot to ring first. My mistake, but I was quizzed by two new gang members who I had not seen before, before I was allowed access. Only when Ronnie came out was I allowed in. Ronnie did not look that great. I could tell his arm was giving him some grief. But the important thing to me was that he was coping with the pain and not going on the wacky baccy to ease his symptoms. He reckoned that Tananga would not let him use the cannabis and he had threatened everyone in the Gang HQ to see him before offering any relief to Ronnie. Now I sat and looked at Tananga, He was a scary dude. I later found out that Tananga ruled his gang with an iron fist and he was not scared to use his fists if anyone disobeyed him.

Ronnie had to go into town and pick up the script from the Doctor. Because he had a Māori name the Chemist was most particular about not releasing morphine to a gang member, even in low doses. Ronnie's trip into town was without incident so it had worked out fine.

Over a brew Ronnie told me he had organised every gang member who was not on active security to go out and start recruiting shopkeepers for security purposes. By this, I mean he was offering protection at $50 per week. I really did not want to hear about this but Ronnie was in a talkative mood, so I listened. On a personal level I might have started in the middle of town, say Hinemoa Street and worked back out towards Arawa Street and Eat Street. That was not the way the Gangs worked. They started at Pukaki Street and moved towards the middle of town. I was happy to listen and also aware that the station would be getting phone calls about these so called 'Security patrols'. At this point, that was not my problem.

Ronnie and Tananga's Boys were better salesmen that their opposition gang members. Within three days they had covered their half of town and were making some inroads into Tohi's part of town. By the Friday I would have thought that Ronnie's territory included most of Eruera Street.

There were several small incidents around town. On one day Ronnie's gang of perhaps six riders were riding along Malfroy Road when one of them looked around and saw they were being followed by a dozen of the opposition Bikers. They turned into a side street, Thebes Street, and gunned their bikes and came to a dead stop about halfway down the road. They then parked their bikes against the kerb on either side forcing the street to become a virtual one way street. They quickly drew their weapons and waited for the opposition gang to enter the street. For whatever reason the opposition gang were headed out to somewhere else so did not follow the six riders into the street. It was just as well because they would have ridden into a deathtrap. We only heard about this from the residents of the street who were obviously concerned about a half dozen gang members riding into their street and dismounting and grabbing shotguns etc to defend themselves. After about a half hour the riders got back on their bikes and rode away as if nothing had happened. That left the residents of the street to start bombarding us with their calls. Also a few of them might have got on to the local paper as they also had full coverage of the incident the next morning.

Another incident arose on Old Quarry Road. Six of the Mongrel mob were getting fish and chips from the Takeaway on OQR when their opposition turned up to get supplies from the Countdown on the same block. It could well have turned nasty, but the Mob were just about ride off with their food and a mini situation de-escalated quickly as the Mob rode away. The BP lot were smart enough to know that now was not the time to start calling them cowards for riding away and what could have been nasty was diffused simply. I wondered why the BP lot were going into Mob territory but the Sarge reckoned they probably had a contact at the Countdown who was giving them food at a discount price. By that I mean they were getting food at a significant discount!

Another incident occurred at the Boozer on Tutanekai St. Evidently the BP lot were unaware that the Mob had entered Eruera St and pinched some of their protection clients. The Mob lads were having a beer at what they thought was in their own territory. A fight broke out. One of the Mob ended up in the A&E dept and was later admitted for surgery on a broken leg. Two of the BP lot were also taken up to the A&E dept for relatively minor cuts that may or may not have involved a knife being drawn. The Squad room lads who were called reckoned it would have been a great all in brawl as some of the locals who were regulars also took exception to the out of towners coming into their pub. They reacted accordingly but none of the regulars were involved in the injury count.

Last, and not the least serious, was a BBQ at one of the gang houses in Western Heights on the Saturday afternoon. I'd have thought this was a Mongrel Mob territory but a family of a gang member were having a few snarlers and a few beers to celebrate how things were going, when a group of six from the BP opposition turned up and started blasting half a dozen Shotguns shells at the assembled gathering. Two of the crowd went down and the rest of the crowd started retaliating by throwing whatever was available at the intruders. Chairs and a table were among the items thrown before the assembled BBQers started mixing it with the BP lot. It possibly only would have gone on for a few minutes before the BP lot got on their bikes and went off up the road and disappeared. When the calm had been restored and the residents got back to their own people it was discovered that two of the people attending had shotgun wounds. One was relatively minor but the other was sufficiently serious to warrant an ambulance being called. They attended to the minor wound while they were on site and then once the other guy had been stabilized they shot him off to hospital. He was in there for four days while they patched him up and of course he was the recipient of a couple of gang members on his door while he was there. He reckoned it gave him some mana for the other patients to know he had been wounded in the gang war that was going on. I was called out on the Saturday afternoon to go and see the BBQ attendees and who should I meet but Tananga!

"Sarge, this is what you call your gang war? Hitting civvies? Some bloke who turns up at a BBQ and gets blasted! Back in the big city we reckon civvies are off limits. I have to tell Ronnie that we start having a go at civvies! If it's good enough for this Tohi bloke, it's good enough for us!"

I immediately started to try and calm him down. I had only just arrived on the scene and been met with Tananga spewing fire at me. "Look, mate. Let's all calm down and see what Ronnie has to say. But before we do that let's see what these lads have to say first. OK?"

I walked around and perhaps a few beers had taken some effect but the general mood was that they had seen the 'Bloody Black power lads off.' All this was said while the ambo's were still tending to the more seriously injured guy on the gurney. I spoke to everyone and got a clear picture that this was definitely a Black Power hit on an innocent BBQ where civilians were involved.

I rang the Boss and got him at home, fortunately. He sounded like he may have had a drink or two. I made the decision to leave him at home, while I first went to see the guy at the hospital and then I would go and see Ronnie and hope that Tananga had not got him all fired up first.

At the hospital I actually met Richard Newberry; the Doctor I had spoken to earlier in the week. He ran his eye over the new patient's form and said, "He's lucky. We probably have at least a couple of dozen pellets in him but I can't see he has any major damage to any organs. Then I went to see the patient. He was just a little out of it with the medication he had been put on. I was trying to speak to him while the nurse or surgeon was trying to get most of the pellets out of him. I didn't get much out of the patient so I left and then went to see Ronnie.

Ronnie had been got at by Tananga. He was fuming when I got there. I'm going to say that, in mitigation, Ronnie did not look great. His face revealed he was in some pain and that only seemed to fuel his anger, which I reckoned was partly due to the pain he was in.

"Civilians, Sarge. Bloody civilians. I don't mind fighting a bloody gang war when it's down to us, But civilians are a no-no. Now the gloves are off.!"

I was trying to get a word in but it was difficult, "Ronnie, Listen to me. Bloody listen to me for a moment!"

I have to say I was thinking on my feet and that is not ever my strongest point. "If you have a go at civilians, who do you think they are going to blame. It might be the Black Power or it might be you lads.

How would you like to be known as the gang leader who waged war on civilians?"

Tananga was adamant it was open warfare and the BP lads had started it, but I was still trying to appeal to Ronnie. I knew he was a fairly decent bloke and wouldn't wage war on the civilians if he thought about it.

Ronnie won out but it was mainly due to my powers of persuasion and the fact that Ronnie was beginning to feel the pain from his wound again. As well as the broken bone, he had also torn completely through his bicep and possibly his triceps as well. Anytime he moved his arm he was in severe pain. Yes he was wearing a sling for his arm but even with that he was still in a lot of pain.

"But Tohi has to be told civilians are not fair game." This was said through Ronnie's gritted teeth.

"I'll get the Boss to give him a rark up but it won't be until tomorrow."

At this Ronnie was angry, "What about today? If he can have a go at our lads today, then it should be okay for your boss to talk to him today."

I looked Ronnie full in the face, "Ronnie. I spoke to the Boss earlier today and he sounds like he is pissed. Do you want him to go and see Tohi when he is pissed?"

Ronnie could turn on his cheeky grin in an instant. He grinned at me," You're right. He should be allowed to get on the piss on his weekend off. But you tell him I want him to be up to see Tohi tomorrow." With that we shook hands. Tananga was teed off but Ronnie was still the boss of the local lads and his word still carried weight. Going to see the Boss was still on the cards but I could handle that if I could handle Ronnie and Tananga.

Leaving the Gang HQ I was surprised to get one of the junior gang lads come down and hustle me back inside.

Ronnie was waiting for me upstairs, "I just had a word with Tohi's number 2. It seems that the incident today had nothing to do with Tohi. If you can believe that! Says it was an accident that civilians got involved and it won't happen again."

I looked at Ronnie to see if he was doubting the sincerity of the message. It seemed like he wasn't as Tananga had answered the phone and spoken to Tohi's 2-I-C. They had a chat for a few seconds and it looks like Tananga had calmed down. Ronnie still wanted me to tell the Boss about having a word with Tohi about civilians being left alone. I agreed with him and left his place to go home. I had a golf game with the Boss tomorrow. I would probably mention it then, hopefully after he had a bad hole or two on his mind. That way I could turn the screw a bit deeper!

<u>Sunday</u>

I had my game with the Sarge and the Boss today. Unfortunately I was the one having the 'not so good day at the Golf Course'. The Sarge won and I came a distant third four strokes behind. The Boss had a good day so I waited until the post-game beer to mention the update on Ronnie and his insistence the Boss tells Tohi that civilians are not supposed to be involved. I think the Boss was happy he had beaten me by three strokes so he took it well.

Oh and I never mentioned anything about my updates on Tinder. I had met a girl named Julie on the Saturday for coffee. I immediately knew that Julie was not the one for me. She was so nervous it was almost embarrassing. She was new to the dating scene having split up with her hubby a few months previous. Her mates had egged her on to try Tinder so she had a go. When she realised I was also new to the dating scene she did calm down a little but she was so nervous, it became something of a joke between us. In mainly men terms I told her what Pauline had told me the previous Saturday and we had a laugh about the whole Tinder scene. We laughed that I was telling her what to do about sex and it was all from the male point of view. We agreed we were not the one for each other and we parted company after about an hour. I got a nice peck on the cheek from her which made me think of Janet and the relationship I had with her. Yes, she was what you might call a 'working girl' but I still felt it was just a little above that level. I decided I should go and see Janet and see if she had any advice for me. All of this was in the brief few seconds after Julie gave me a peck on the cheek. I have to get out and see more Tinder ladies!

<u>Monday</u>

Bernie was in on the Monday as she had finished her weekend shift rotation. Derek was on that duty for next weekend and the following three weekends. I still got some ribbing from the Sarge and the Boss about my Tinder update. Fortunately I was able to report that nothing had happened. The Boss reckoned I should ask for my money back. The Sarge reckoned I was wasting my time. What if I looked at some of the new WPC on the staff?. At least that way they would know what the copper's life is like. The Boss reminded him that I had already gone down that path and the Sarge just said, "Oh, yeah."

We all sat down in the bull pen and had a recap from the Boss and I about what had gone down the previous week. In particular I spent some time explaining what had happened on the Saturday afternoon with the BBQ in Western Heights. I explained in some detail about how Tananga had reacted and then calmed down when he had got the call from Tohi's second in command on the Saturday afternoon. Evidently there was honour among the thieves we were up against.

The Sarge allocated the Jobs from the Squad room and there was a case that Bernie wanted to follow up on from the weekend so she was allowed to carry on with that one while Mike and I got to deal with the other cases that arose.

The Boss had nothing to do so he supposed he had better get out to see Tohi. I went out on two cases. One was a retail burglary and one was a domestic assault which always took priority. The domestic assault was an on odd one. He had beaten her up and that was not good. However it had occurred at a friend's house and they were the ones putting in the complaint as they reckoned the hubby may have done it before. When I got there to Fairview Road the wife who had been beaten up was already there along with the complainant. It seems like I was fated to intervene in this couple's married bliss as it was the woman I had spoken to last week, the one who would not press charges. I do have the power to press charges, as in 'the Police can press charges' if they decided to.

The woman had the usual amount of bruises as this had only happened on the Sunday afternoon. I was fairly convinced that the Law should press charges, even if we were busy with other things such as the Gang war and the rapist. I told the wife that we were going to press charges and for some reason she insisted she wanted to press charges. Maybe she thought that if she pressed the charge for battery she could always withdraw the charge and she might have a few months of non-battery or violence against her. I told her that we would also press charges and if she withdrew her charges we would still continue to press the charges. It was a sobering thought for the wife as she realised she should not have to deal with this kind of assault whenever the hubby got drunk.

I took the statement from the wife and also one from the complainant. Then I asked a squad car to go to the guy's work and arrest him on a charge of battery or assault. By the time I got back to the station, the wife and kids were organised to move in with the complainant. She had booked an appointment with a solicitor to start divorce proceedings and I had the guy in custody. I hate to say it but nobody should be expected to live with the constant threat of drunken violence, but it does seem to be something we have to deal with nowadays.

I also dealt with the retail burglary. It was a shop on Eruera St and the bright spark in charge of the shop asked me if he should go for a claim against the insurance or one against the Black Power lads. He was under the impression that he could also claim against them. I suggested he might be better consulting with the Insurance company and left him to it. People that stupid should be left alone to their own devices.

I went up to see Ronnie and Tananga. Ronnie looked a little better. He said the pain from the broken arm was improving and even the lower strength morphine pills seemed to be doing him some good in the area of pain relief. So far he had kept off the wacky baccy but that may have had something to do with the presence of Tananga.

I noticed there were a few less lads in the Mob HQ. Ronnie said a number of them had gone home to their own territory. They had made a statement to Tohi's Mob by showing up in support of Ronnie and they would be back in a few hours if Tohi showed signs of getting 'cheeky' again. I spoke to Ronnie and Tananga. It's a delicate subject but I will venture to probe a bit that way. Ronnie was saying he was missing his missus but the lads had arranged it so that he did not feel too lonely. Is that delicate enough? Tananga also said he was missing his woman but he preferred only Māori working girls. He had found one that he really liked so she was becoming a regular visitor to the Mob HQ. I found it just a bit odd that this was a subject so freely talked about. I would say it was something that I found a little odd but these lads were the best part of fifteen or twenty years younger than me so who am I to say what is right for them at their age.

It got me to thinking about the Tinder app and I wondered whether I should have another go at it. So far I had met three girls and we were not ideal for each other. Maybe it was just part of keeping trying until you found one that fits you. That sounds better in my head than it does on paper!

I thought I might try another go on Tinder that night and resolved to try again. Then I remembered I had promised to visit Janet sometime this week. Well I could always do both!

That night I did go on Tinder and met a lady, Maureen, who would like a drink the next night. I agreed and we set up a time to meet and I looked at her photo for a while. She looked nice in her picture.

Tuesday

In at my usual time and the weather was glorious. It looked like it could be this good for the rest of the week. The Sarge had my coffee ready for me and I sat down to drink it. The Sarge and I had a chat. Bernie was taking a couple of days off because she worked the weekend. Derek wasn't supposed to start until the Wednesday morning and I had no idea where Mike and the Boss were.

The Sarge and I were having a chat about a variety of subjects when the Boss and Mike walked in. it seems that the two of them had been called out earlier for a homicide in Malfroy Road. Well just off it in Pandora. There was no link with the gang war so I had been left out of this one as I was supposed to be fully focused on the Gang war. The Boss and Mike had been called out at a little after six this morning. From what they could see it was a burglar and the quiet entry had gone awry. The victim was home when he should have been away for the evening. There had been a struggle and the victim had been walloped over the head with a meat tenderizer. Not to belittle the assailant but it just happened to be the nearest weapon to hand. But the victim had suffered repeated blows and as a result had passed away. Now the Boss and Mike were looking for clues. The print lads were doing their thing as we spoke so the Boss and Mike had come away to have some breakfast and regroup.

I so wanted to tell somebody about my date tonight but the Sarge never gave me the opportunity and then the Boss and Mike walked in so I kept it to myself. Perhaps I reckoned if I was not quite so secretive about my love life it might take a turn for the better. Anyway I kept it to myself for the time being.

The phone rang around 11.30am and it was Shi Low asking me to call around for a cup of tea. Tomorrow at 2.00pm would be convenient.

I was out doing the Squad room cases we had been handed on. I had a couple of commercial burglaries to deal with. The first one was pretty much like the second one. It was a machine shop that did motorcycle repairs and ride on mower repairs etc. A whole load of spare parts had been taken. Given we had a gang war in progress it didn't take much to realise that it could have been either of the gangs who was the guilty party. There were accessories that would have easily been recognizable in Town but not if they were flicked off in another town like Auckland. Also there were other items that could loosely be described as maintenance items - replacement oil, gaskets for the more popular types of Harley Davidson. Oil filters etc.

No, it didn't really warrant that much brain power to work out who were the likely crims involved. Sadly, I could not really even say whether it was Ronnie's Mob or Tohi's mob who were the guilty party. It could have been either of them! I satisfied myself by believing it was probably one of the out of town visitors. I did the usual thing of taking photos and getting the fingerprint lads out. Beyond that there wasn't a lot for me to do.

I debated whether or not to go to Janet's in the afternoon. If I had just had sex I would not be quite so keen for my date this evening. I decided not to and I would be fresh and ready for anything when I met 'what was her name', Maureen? I'd better not make that mistake tonight!

I went up to see Ronnie and Tananga in the afternoon and The Boss went to see Tohi. Nothing really to report. Tohi was pissed off at the way Ronnie had got everyone on his team to work on increasing their protected area. Tohi reckoned he might have had a week to get it organised. Now he was left with definitely the smaller side of town.

The Boss still reckoned Tohi may have something on his plans for Ronnie but he was not having any success in getting Tohi to confide in him. I went to see Ronnie and Ronnie was obviously in pain but he was struggling through the pain and finally making some clear headed decisions. For me I was thrilled to see Ronnie back at his best or at least very near to his best. Tananga reckoned he would only need to stay for a few more days if Ronnie was recovering this well.

I may have slipped away just a little early from work. I reckoned with all of this warm weather, another shower would not do me any harm and a rest before meeting Maureen might also be in order.

I met Maureen at the CT club and she was right on time. As was I.

I think it might have been Pauline who suggested if I turned up too early it looked like I was desperate. Whatever, we had a few drinks together and she asked me to drop her off at her house on Otonga Road. I was happy to oblige and she also asked me in for a cuppa. I might as well finish the evening off with a cuppa so I went inside.

Once she was inside her whole attitude changed. She asked me if I wanted sex. I said yes, more in optimism than hope. Within a very few seconds we were naked and on her bed. She lived alone, fortunately, as I discovered later. It didn't really occur to me make that enquiry when we were both stripping each other off. After our first somewhat frenetic bout of sex we cuddled for a moment or two before she got the idea that I was ready for more. I was quickly on top, but she shoved me off so I immediately thought I had done something wrong. As usual I was ready to apologise but while pushing me off her she somehow managed to get on top of me and she was, can I say an active participant? No it was more than that, she was an enthusiastic participant. Her enthusiasm might have made me get just touch more excited than normal and I was finished a good deal before she was. She looked at me with something akin to disappointment, so we lay down next to each other and talked about any number of things before I knew I was not going to rise to the occasion again tonight. Now don't get me wrong but she er... finished herself off while I was laying on the bed alongside her. Actually, I lay alongside her and watched the whole thing. I was amazed that was how the girls treated sex nowadays. Definitely it was something that both sides were expected to enjoy. She laughed it off and we got out of bed and had a cup of tea. She was doing it mainly for the sex. She could have it away with a guy and it was really down to her whether she saw the guy again. If he was good in bed she might see him again. If not, then it was still her choice.

She reminded me a little of Janet with her attitude to sex, although Janet was a giver and a taker whereas Maureen was definitely more of a taker.

We agreed to see each other again but left without anything definite arranged. I might be a little insecure but to me that meant I would not hear from Maureen again. But then again, you never know!

Wednesday

And the weather reflected my mood. Very sunny!

I wanted to drop into the conversation that I had sex last night and with one of the Tinder ladies! But somehow the situation didn't present itself for at least a half hour! I might have subtly mentioned it to the Sarge. Who then might have mentioned it to the Boss. Who might have mentioned it to Mike and Derek. Before I knew it I was getting knowing looks from everybody. Even the Sarge from the Squad room gave me a nod. By now I knew I was getting a bit paranoid. Nobody really cared if I was getting it regular as they all had their own lives and problems to deal with. FOWOPTOM the Boss had called it and he was right. Most people had their own problems to deal with in preference to being bothered about what was going on in your life.

I settled down to my day. The Sarge gave me a domestic burglary to deal with as the other two, Mike and Derek, were also busy on something hanging around from Mike's case on the previous day. Bernie was still on her days off so I went to deal with the domestic burglary. It was in Basley Road and a motorcycle had been stolen. It was only a 250 CC Kawasaki so I could be reasonably safe in discounting either of the gangs being the villain. It was something the owner's lad had used when he was going up and down the trails in the nearby Whaka Forest. Such a small machine would have been laughed at if they had turned up at the Gang HQ. The owner had the keys inside the house so the Crim or crims had wheeled it away and then hotwired it when they were out of earshot. They had also grabbed whatever was in the carport at the place although the guy reckoned it wouldn't have added up to more than few hundred dollars' worth of mower and petrol tank etc. I got the fingerprint lads out to do what they could but I didn't have much hope unless the crims repeated the offence.

I diverted on the way back to the Station and went up to see Ronnie. For a joke I stopped at the Fruiteries on Hinemoa St and got some grapes. Ronnie was in a much better mood nowadays and he would appreciate the joke.

I rang Ronnie from the Fruit Shop and told them I was coming. So when I arrived at the gang HQ I was expected and, after a cursory glance, the car was rolled from the inside and I was let in.

I gave the grapes to Ronnie and he roared with laughter. Tananga reckoned the only thing he had ever got from their local cops was when he got a summons while he was in his hospital bed and that was for speeding.

We sat down and had a brew and we enjoyed the grapes as well. Tananga reckoned he would go back to Auckland on the weekend seeing as Tohi seemed to be behaving himself and Ronnie was just about back to his usual self. I had got reasonably friendly with Tananga as I had needed his help with Ronnie. I'd be sorry to see Tananga go. He told me his real name was Tanahanga but as a kid he had never been able to pronounce his name correctly so Tananga had stuck as his first name. It was odd to think that in our early days Tananga had been quite reserved when it came to the local law lads. Now he was sat down with me and we were enjoying a joke or two. Maybe I had made some inroads as to how we did things differently away from the Big City.

I went back to the Station and was reminded by the Sarge that I had a meeting with Shi Low at 2.00PM. I sat and ate my lunch and waited for 2pm to roll around.

I was exactly on time as I walked up the stairs to Shi Low's outer rooms. I was immediately ushered in and shown through to Shi Low's office. I was welcomed informally and offered tea. This was something of a ritual between us. Sipping the tea gave us some breathing space to come up with an answer to a tricky question.

As we settled down in our comfortable chairs Shi Low broached the subject he wanted to discuss.

"Detective Sergeant. I have heard that you have the makings of a gang war on our streets."

I was well aware that there was not a lot that went on that Shi Low did not already know about.

I replied. "Yes. There is some ill feeling between rival gang members but it should not concern your people."

"Detective Sargeant, I understand that some of the members of these gangs have visited some of the local businesses and offered them some form of protection if they were to pay a nominal fee."

I explained myself a little more clearly. With Shi Low it was better to be clear although I have to say his language difficulties were not something I ever had a problem with. "Shi Low, allow me to explain or expand things to make them easier. I am in daily consultation with one of the gangs, the Mongrel Mob. I visit with them on a nearly daily basis to make sure our intentions are clear. I constantly urge them to settle their differences and we are making some progress. My superior Detective Inspector Woods is visiting the other gang members, the Black Power, to urge them to be civilised."

Shi Low interrupted," Yet we have these gang members who are going into our people's businesses and offering them the protection that they surely do not need."

Again I tried to be emphatic without being too one sided. "Shi Low, we have known each other for over seven years. I would hope my word can be trusted when I say I have advised the Mongrel Mob members to stay away from your people. Indeed I have even gone so far as to advise them which shops are already offered protection by your own people."

"So you would have no problem if any such person came into one of my people's shops and I dealt with them by saying I already offer protection to my people." Shi Low was looking at me as he made this enquiry. I could only be positive in saying that the Mongrel Mob wouldn't or shouldn't be going into Shi Low's shops if they were smart. He appreciated my comment about the Mob members being smart.

I got the feeling that Shi Low was not telling me something but I was loathe to ask him to elaborate. Between us it was expected we should know everything it was deemed necessary to know. I drank my cup of tea and wished Shi Low all good wishes as I left. It was a formality but I had the feeling I would be hearing more from this meeting. It was a nagging feeling I had but it was there!

I got back to the station and spent the rest of the day reading reports and memos from Divisional HQ. It somehow suited my mood at the time.

Chapter 5

<u>T</u>**<u>hursday</u>**
Another lovely day and my mood was the same. Perhaps not quite so perky as the previous day but I was still in a good mood. I had thought about going to see Janet on the drive into the office. Perhaps I would do that if the day didn't turn out too busy. The Sarge gave me a coffee as I walked into the office. Bernie was already there as well. I mentally told myself I should not be that busy if Derek and Mike and Bernie were all in today. Maybe I will go and see Janet.

The Sarge handed out the cases from the Squad room. I ended up with a case along with Bernie, as in we went to a case together.

It was a case of damage or vandalism. Someone had shoved a rubbish bin through a shop window. The Police had been called as the insurance companies were reluctant to do anything without a Police file number to reference. The owner of the premises was bleating about how he had turned down the offer of protection from the Gangs and he reckoned this was their way of saying he should reconsider their offer. It was in the Mongrel mob part of town so if the owner was correct it should be something the Mob and Ronnie should be aware of.

I made a mental note to mention it to Ronnie when I went to see him later. Driving back to the station Bernie mentioned that I had got lucky the other night with one of the Tinder girls. I almost drove off the road but Bernie was talking about it in a way that she might also be looking for a bit of comfort for herself. I still thought that it was a bit off that Bernie knew about my success. I tried to divert the attention from my being successful by asking her about herself. She said she was getting over a breakup from her ex hubby. It seems he had been messing around with another woman in the South Island. She took the opportunity to get away from him by grabbing the chance to head to the North Island and start a new life. They had no kids so it would be a nice clean break once they had gone through the divorce proceedings. She told me all about herself. She was 38 and quite athletic. She said she had been a contender for the Olympics back in the day as a runner but she had dipped out and it was just another excuse for the hubby to say she was a failure. I looked at her out of the side of my eyes, my peripheral vision, if you like. She was quite attractive in a slim manner if you liked that physique. I didn't reckon she would have any problems finding a bloke on Tinder and I gave her the advice I had passed on to me by Pauline on my first Tinder date.

By that time we had arrived back at the station and I went into report to the Boss. Once I had completed the case paperwork I decided I would go and see Ronnie.

I rang first, as always, and went up to see Ronnie. Ronnie was not looking that good. He had a relapse and as I was talking to him and getting a little concerned about his state of mind, Maggie, the District nurse came to see him. After a few moments she quickly arranged for an ambulance and had him whisked up to the hospital. It seems that Ronnie had developed an infection in his wound and would need the surgeon to operate on him again. I asked Tananga what he could do and he agreed that Ronnie would probably be back in hospital for a few days so he had better stay here until Ronnie was back in charge and making good decisions.

I left the Gang HQ and went to see Ronnie at the hospital. He was already in the surgical ward and under the surgeon's knife by the time I got there. I left the hospital and went back to the Station.

I rang Janet as I had nothing else to do and she said she could see me shortly after 2.00. I had lunch with the Sarge and the Boss and wandered off to do my thing with Janet at the appointed time. I always liked Janet. She had an easy way about her and I always felt comfortable around her. At some time in the next hour I might have mentioned the fact that I was going on Tinder. As far as Janet was concerned she was thrilled for me. We did not have any claims on each other. She liked the idea of sex with different guys and I always found her very warm to me. It was the ultimate friends with benefits arrangement. Okay, I did pay, most of the time!

She did ask me why I went on Tinder and it sounded lame when I said it was because of something that Ronnie had said to me.

I don't know, Maybe it was the halftime interval, you know what I mean! But that was when we usually had a cuddle and a chat. She immediately stopped and turned to me. She said, 'So now I have to get you ready to date."

When I asked her what she meant, she looked at me cryptically and said I had to change my ways. Not a lot but perhaps just a little bit.

From then on my relationship with Janet changed a little. Now I had to practice being a seducer and not just being the guy who expected sex in exchange for a few dollars, and she was determined to teach me ways to improve.

Okay, we were already naked and in bed but she showed me how to go about pleasing a partner. She literally took my hand and put it in the right position where a lady may appreciate the gesture. She showed me so much in the next half hour that it felt like I was taking my exam again for the Senior Sarge. Don't get me wrong but I had always treated Janet like we were going to have sex and it was, for the most part, a lot of fun. Now I had to please the woman as part of being a seducer and it was getting a whole lot harder.

I did appreciate Janet's efforts and she reckons it was very enjoyable for her but I had my doubts. When we were dressed she reckoned that the next time I came to visit her she wanted the whole seduction thing from me. Part of me was a little concerned but a part of me was also looking forward to my next lesson.

From Janet's I went straight up to see Ronnie. He was out of the operating room but still quite groggy so I left him alone. Already, the same nurse was having the same argument with a couple of Ronnie's lads who had been sent to supervise his visitors. I did ask the nurse how long would Ronnie be staying up in the ward. She said four days while they checked the wound was clean. Ronnie's mate reckoned it would only be overnight. The nurse pointed at Ronnie's mate and said she would decide when Ronnie left the ward and if Ronnie's mate had any other ideas he could take it up with the Sister in Charge. I reckoned Ronnie would be up there for at least three days. We would see who was closest.

I went home. All in all it had been a good day.

<u>Friday</u>

It's my fault. I had meant to go on Tinder and tee up another date for Saturday night. But last night I had been caught up with techniques that would make me a better person in bed. That sounds crass! What I meant to say was I spent some time... No, if it sounds crass, it probably was. I was looking for better techniques to please a woman in bed. So much had changed since I was a young guy. Now it was all on the internet and it varied if you were into the skilled application of a variety of vegetables if that was your thing. No, I had to concentrate on my job as a copper and I would leave the training to Janet. Maybe? Actually I was quite looking forward to Janet's training. Would she be naked or would I have to do the whole seduction thing. Either way I was happy.

It was another lovely day and I was thinking of the day ahead when Bernie caught up with me in the car park. She said, "Thanks for the Info you gave me yesterday. I had a go at Tinder last night. It looks like I already have a 100 guys who want to take a chance on me."

"Good luck with Tinder. When I had a go, I had over 100 but when I really looked I managed to get it down to a dozen or so. Even then I had mixed results."

With that we entered the station and I peeled off to where the Sarge was waiting for me with a coffee. He was getting very good at his barista stuff. Either that or the pod machine was doing all of the work. I sat down with the Sarge and the Boss joined us shortly.

"What's the latest on Ronnie and the Mob?" asked the Boss.

"Ronnie is still up in hospital. Last I heard he had his op and they cleaned the whole thing up. Reckon he might have caught an infection from the bullet but they won't know until he gets better. Tananga is still in charge on View Road. I'll go and see him today. How's it going with Tohi?"

"Tohi is still trying to play it cagey. I reckon he is up to something but I can't find out what it is. Everything is quiet on View Road?"

"Yeah. Tananga is waiting to see what happens with Tohi before he reacts. He says he still has to remember that Ronnie is in charge so he is waiting for Ronnie before he does anything that might be seen by Ronnie as a bit cheeky."

The Sarge had been listening into the conversation and he nodded in recognition of the Duty Sarge coming over from the Squad room to pass on anything that CIB should be taking an interest in.

I ended up with a domestic burglary on Pandora Ave. There were five of us in the squad room so Mike and Derek and Bernie got a case each. I said I would go and see Tananga after I had dealt with my case. The Boss said he would go and see Tohi later in the morning. Just then the big Boss walked into our CIB room so the Boss and he disappeared into the Boss's office.

I had just had a coffee so I didn't really need to go and say hi to the Boss and then go upstairs for a cuppa. That was a shame, as I needed an excuse to go and tell the big Boss good morning and go upstairs for a half hour. Maybe I was just in that kind of mood.

I went off to my domestic burglary in Pandora Avenue. The residents had been away for the evening and when they got back just before midnight discovered they had been burgled. Tim Cross had gone up to see them but was then called away on a GBH which was the reason I had been asked to go and see them 9 hours later. I called the fingerprint lads in and assured the occupants we would be doing everything we could to catch these offenders. For those of you who know, that meant I would be adding their names to the list of the burglary victims and hoping we may get a break if they were repeat offenders.

While I was out I made a call to Tananga and went up there to see him.

He already had a report from the two lads at the hospital. They reckoned he would be in for at least three if not four days. According to the nurse it was all down to Ronnie going home a day early during his initial visit when he first went under the surgeon's knife.

Tananga looked a little displeased. He had already been on the phone to his lady friend in Auckland and she was expecting him that weekend. Now he looked like it was going to be the middle of the week at the earliest before he got home.

Tananga was happy enough that he had everything at the Mob HQ in order. If Tohi did not start anything he could keep View Road ticking over until Ronnie got back.

On the way back to the station I called in to see Ronnie. Ronnie was still in a little pain, but despite that, he remained cheered to see me.

"Hey, Sarge. It's okay if you feel the need to bring me a few grapes again. There is no limit on how often I can get grapes."

I shook Ronnie's hand and I was genuinely pleased to see him looking a bit more chipper than when I had seen him yesterday. I reported that Tananga was coping ok and as far as I could tell, Tohi was still behaving himself. We chatted for a few minutes and then I left him to get some rest.

Going back to the station I was met by the Sarge as I entered the CIB room. "I'm getting a report that some of the Black Power lads might have gone to see some of Shi Low's business owners. I don't think they got a great reception. Shi Low and you have a good rapport. Is it worth you going to see him?"

That put me slightly on the back foot. I quickly weighed up the pros and cons of having a meeting with Shi Low and decided against it. "Shi Low said he would be concerned if any of the Mob lads went to see the Chinese and I told him that would not happen. Let's see if I get a call from Shi Low and we'll play it by ear. You sure it was the Black Power lads and not the Mob?"

"That's what I am hearing. Definitely the Black Power lads."

Just then the Boss walked back into the CIB room. "I've just heard that some of Tohi's lads went into one of the Chinese shops and offered them protection."

I had to ask, "And how did they take it?"

"The owner kept them talking until Shi Low's lads arrived."

"And then what happened?"

"The Black Power lads kept insisting they needed protection. Shi Low's lads insisted that Shi Low could offer protection to his own people. Then it got a bit messy."

"How messy?"

"Well they were big lads from the BP lot, but they were still no match for Shi Low's lot. Last I heard they broke the fingers of the Black Power mob. The way I heard it was that they might have broken a couple of fingers. Tohi reckons it's an insult they cannot let go unpunished. I reckoned that Shi Low was best left alone, and any of his shopkeepers might be better left alone. I tried to make the point but Tohi is an odd bugger."

I had to add, "The last thing we need is for Shi Low to get involved."

"That's down to Tohi to sort out. Anything else to report?" he asked the Sarge and me. I reported on Ronnie's progress and reckoned he may be in three for at least three, if not four days. The Boss was happy enough and I asked him why.

"One, I have Shi Low's lads giving Tohi's lot the message. Two, I have a half hour golf lesson with the pro at Springfield. You can come if you want. Oh, sorry, Sarge, not you. That's what you get for taking every bloody Saturday and Sunday off while we are slaving away in the office. Cheers. Well come on then, you might need your clubs if you are getting a free lesson on me." With that the Boss turned and left the office. I looked at the Sarge and then also left the office. I was only a minute behind the Boss as he drove up to the golf course.

The Boss had been watching all of the YouTube videos on getting your drive away in a straight line. I was just a bit pleased he had opened the lesson to include me as well. Within a few moments we were down to the practice driving range and hitting golf balls, and listening to the tips the pro was handing out. For the Boss, the pro reckoned the Boss's shoulder was way too far from square as he addressed the ball. For me he reckoned I had my right shoulder too low as I entered the backswing. Within a half hour we were hitting a reasonably straight drive with woods and irons. The pro reckoned we were starting our swing at odd angles. Once he had us correct that, we were doing well.

The pro reckoned we should both be playing off below an eighteen handicap as we had the basics in good order but just needed some fine tuning.

I was mentally preparing myself for Sunday's game with the Boss and the Sarge and wondering how easy this game really could be.

That night I went home and booked a date for tomorrow night. The Citizens club at 7.30pm and I was meeting Julieana. She looked fairly foxy on her photo so I was quite looking forward to meeting Julieana.

Saturday.

I received a phone call from Tananga. It must have been before 9.00 am as I wondered why he would be ringing me at that hour.

Tananga reckoned he had a phone call from some Chink. (His words, not mine) saying if we wanted to talk to a couple of lads they were at this address. As the address was up at the Otonga Road shops I wondered why I had to be involved. Tananga explained, " Look I just got a call from some guy who sounded like he was a Chink. Could have been Asian but he reckons I would want to talk to these lads. I said I wasn't interested so he said he would leave them there until we were interested. I dunno. Send one of your squaddies around to see if they are worth talking to." With that he hung up. I assume he had got my phone number from Ronnie's phone. By now I was interested in the call. I rang into the CIB room and Derek was on duty. I told him about the call I had just received so he sent a squad car to check it out.

Within ten minutes he was back on the phone to me." DS, I reckon you should meet those lads you were talking about. The ambulance is just about there. Give it a half hour and they should be at the hospital.

Okay, so my curiosity was piqued.

I drove up to the Otonga Shops and I had to back out from the driveway as I risked blocking the ambulance in. I parked the car and wandered around the back of the shops. There were a couple of lads who did not look too healthy propped up against the wall. I spoke to the ambos and he reckoned they had just got there themselves. As much as he could say was that these lads had been severely beaten as a form of torture. They would be available at the hospital in perhaps an hour. Till then I should let the ambos get on with their job!

I left the scene and went back to the station. So much for my lie in!

I had a coffee with Derek. The Sarge made a slightly better cup than me but the machine did all of the work. I also noted that Derek was having a coffee. Last I heard he had not chipped in for the machine but that was not my current problem.

I had breakfast in the staff canteen and it was not bad at all. Then I went up to the hospital to see the two guys who were now in A&E.

As soon as I walked in they both confessed to having a go at Ronnie some three weeks ago. I knew I could not take their word for it as any statement made under duress would be quickly thrown out of court.

However these lads were adamant they should confess. When I looked at them they were a mess. Both had a couple of lost fingernails. I could imagine them having a bike accident but they were the same fingers on the same hand. That was too much of a coincidence. I spoke to the nurse who was tidying their various injuries and she also thought that had been tortured or at least 'professionally' interrogated. At the back of my mind I had a feeling that Shi Low may have had something to do with it but I pushed that thought to the back of my mind.

I said I would leave them alone for an hour or so but they were adamant they had done the crime on Ronnie. When I asked them who was the shooter one of them owned up straight away and the other guy reckoned he drove the getaway bike. He reckoned if you had just topped someone you were not fit to ride a bike, or in this case a motorcycle.

I left the room and rang the Boss. I was not that keen to hear the Boss's dulcet tones if I had disturbed his sleep but he was quite chirpy as he spoke on the phone. I explained the situation and said I had a couple of Black Power lads confessing to the crime of shooting Ronnie. At first he said I had done a good job until I explained about evidence gathered under duress. He said he would be there in a half hour. I stayed out of the room where the two lads were being treated. I had a confession to an attempted murder but I could not use it!

The Boss arrived half an hour later. He took one look at the two lads and he also reckoned we would not be able to use their confession. He got on the phone to someone. I later found out it was the Crown Prosecutor and asked how long would it be before we could use the confession. As far as the CP was concerned we couldn't use anything until at least twelve hours after they had been taken into the A&E, and after that we would need the CP to be on top form to avoid the evidence being thrown out of court. I suggested to the Boss that we could leave it until this time tomorrow and then it would not stuff up my date with Julieana. So, I like to look at the big picture.

The Boss reckoned we had a game booked for tomorrow. How about we let Derek handle these lads tomorrow and see what he could get out of them?

We agreed on that as the best course and we left the two lads being treated for a myriad of cuts and bruises. I thought later that this could be the origin of 'death by a thousand cuts'. They had certainly been well worked over and by a professional questioner or torturer. At that point I could not really decide which.

That evening I met with Julieana. Yes, it's an odd way of spelling her name but that is the name she wanted to use. I might be an intellectual snob but Julieana was a bit dim! She seemed to agree with everything I said. When I asked her about herself she seemed a little confused and gave vague answers. She probably would have agreed to anything I suggested. She was a nice looking lady but I just had the impression that the lift did not go all the way to the top floor. We chatted and had a couple of drinks but there was little attraction from me and I reckon she probably picked up the same vibe from me. Oh and I paid for all of the drinks. It's not a big issue but again I was left wondering who paid for what in modern society. I think if I had suggested we finish the night off with sex she would have agreed because she seemed to agree with everything I said. I didn't make that suggestion and we parted friends. I was home before 10pm and I settled down and watched the box until I fell asleep.

Chapter 6

S<u>unday</u>

I was quite looking forward to our game on the Sunday. I was keen to put to use the advice I had been given by the pro. I got in my usual ten minutes of practice on the putting green and I was ready for when we teed off. It was just the three of us today. The Sarge was already practicing his excuses if he did not have a great day. He mentioned something about having to work for a living while his colleagues swanned off and had golf lessons. It was good natured but I was still keen to give my new swing set up a good go.

I drew the honors on the first tee, and I sent it straight down the middle of the fairway and probably within twenty meters of the green. I walked back to my bag while muttering 'still twenty meters short of the green. Maybe I should hold my left shoulder a bit higher.' To an outsider I sounded like a pro wondering why I was still twenty yards short of the green. At least that is what I was hoping for. The Boss took out his driver and said something to the effect of 'in your bloody dreams it will work!'

He drove his tee shot horribly into the rough on the right hand side. I replied, " And in your dreams that worked out a lot better, didn't it?" The Boss was disappointed but he still managed a grin until he went looking for the ball and didn't find it. Then his grin was replaced by a scowl.

The Sarge put his tee shot down the middle and about thirty meters short of mine.

I won the first hole with a fluke of a birdie and wandered off to the second tee and waited for my two colleagues to hole out.

I won the day but only by a single shot and the Boss and the Sarge were in equal second. I don't think the golf lesson helped that much but it was an exciting way to play with each of us with an outside chance of winning every hole. I ended up with a 99 and the other two got a 100. I somehow still won on the handicap system and the Sarge worked it all out so I had a free beer for my efforts.

The Boss and I went via the CIB room on our way home to see if our two lads in A&E had said anything more to Derek. They had virtually repeated what they had said to us the previous day. They had both been admitted to a ward as their condition overall was suffering from a multitude of cuts and abrasions and the nurses were concerned about their overall health. One other deciding factor was that these two lads were happy either in the ward under a police guard or in the cells under a police guard. They most definitely did not want to be released under bail. The whole thing was very odd but that was a problem for tomorrow.

I had done a half hour on the Tinder thing before my golf game this morning and I had a reply from one of the Tinder ladies. The net result was I had a date at the CT club for a drink at 7.30pm. Part of me was pleased but a small part of me was quite happy that I had won the golf game and had my celebratory drink.

As usual I was there on time at the CT club and I wandered in. My lady was not there and I didn't want to get a drink for myself so I sat and waited. Her name was Hazel and she was supposed to be wearing a pinkish jumper. I sat for five minutes and waited until my heart sank. Bernie had walked in, from the office.

I felt my heart slide. The last thing I wanted to see was Bernie. Don't get me wrong, she was a very attractive lady but if she and I were on our Tinder dates in the same club, it could be awkward.

Bernie walked over to me and sat down.

She opened with, "So how does this work then? Do I buy you a drink or do you buy me one?"

I was just a little flustered, "Oh, hi, Bernie. You on a Tinder date?"

"Yes, with you! Don't you ever look at the picture before you make a date?"

I was on autopilot and just a little concerned that she would see me with my date, so I said. "Oh, yeah, can I get you a drink or something? Hang on. In your photo you had longer hair."

"Yes. That was taken last year. I had my hair cut shorter when I got back into running again. You don't like me with long hair?"

"No, as in yes, I reckon your hair looks great. I didn't mean to er.... Infer that your hair was... different."

She looked at me and then said she would like an orange juice as she did not normally drink.

I went up to the bar and ordered a beer for myself and an orange juice for Bernie. I sat and watched her out of the corner of my eye. She was quite attractive. I'd have said she was a bit young for me. She was only, did she say she was 38 or was it 39? I was trying to remember the conversation we had in my car. I'm sure she said she was 39. I was 46 or was it just turned 47. While I was waiting for the guy to get my drinks order there was a whole raft of thoughts going on in my head. I had put in my search form I was looking for 40 to 50 year old. Maybe they put in a year either side as part of the search. Similar interests? Well she probably ticked that box as we were both coppers, and we were both interested in solving crimes.

The guy behind the bar served me my drinks. I paid and then walked back to Bernie carrying the drinks. I have to say she was as nervous as I was.

First we both started talking and then we both shut up to let the other one speak. Then in the awkward pause we both started talking again. It was not off to a great start.

We both stopped talking again. Then she started with, "Look I don't know what you are looking for on Tinder but here we both are.

At the very least it's a girl and a guy having a drink together. Can we get past the awkward stage and work on that much?"

I agreed. I asked her about her life since she had come to Rotorua from the deep south. She said she had enjoyed moving north. At least the weather was usually warmer. She had a flat on Pandora Ave which was fine until she decided she wanted to stay in Rotorua. I didn't know that she was only looking at Rotorua as a stopgap until she decided where she wanted to be. That was a bit of a downer for me. I quite liked working with her. She had an energy about her.

We talked a little uncomfortably for a while and then we started to relax a little more. She was fun to be with. She had a good sense of humour and she was certainly attractive.

We spoke for a while. I offered to get more drinks but she insisted she would pay for them and she got up and went off to the bar and ordered them. I watched her walk away and I was a little surprised at how attractive she really was. Maybe it was me being overreactive to not dating another lady from the law but I had not really noticed her before. She was quite attractive.

She turned around and headed back to our table with the drinks she had purchased.

"So what happens now?" she asked.

I queried her.

She was quite blunt, "Well I don't know if I am ready for sex with you. By the looks of you, you aren't that sure, either?"

In the deep south of the South Island they are evidently just a little blunter with their speech.

She continued, "Well, do we see each other again or just go out for a drink, occasionally."

She had a refreshingly blunt way of speaking.

I replied, "Well I would like to see you again. I don't also know about sex. Not that I don't know about sex. It's just that, well sex is something to talk about later."

She was laughing with me now. "You don't seem this nervous when you are speaking to the lot of us in the bull pen. Or is it just when you get nervous talking about sex. You're in charge of the vice squad aren't you? That can't be a lot of help when you are talking to the girls, the working girls!"

I was stuck for an answer.

She replied as if she had made an internal decision. The decision was not in my favour or so it seemed. "Okay. Well I have to go. It's been great seeing you. Maybe you will click on my page on Tinder again."

I had to stop her from leaving. "No. Don't go. Yes, I really do want to see you again. Have another drink!"

I was getting flustered and it seemed the more I spoke, the more flustered I got. "Please stay for a while. Sex we can talk about later but only when you want to talk about it and how are we going to handle this tomorrow?"

She had a quick reply, "Well for a start you can do us both a favour by not mentioning everything to the Sarge when you have your coffee together like you usually do."

I agreed.

"Well the next thing to sort out is if you want to meet me again and when?"

"Next Saturday. No make it next Wednesday, here at the CT. Is 7.30 ok with you?"

"Okay, last question. I haven't called you anything since I got here. Can I call you Mark when we are alone?"

"Not a problem and I have a question for you. You call yourself Hazel. What is that about?"

"That's an easy one. I was told by the great seducer not to use my real name on Tinder. Hazel is a mate of mine in Invercargill."

"Who is the great seducer?"

"That's you, you idiot. Since you got loose on Tinder all of the married blokes are jealous. You are getting sex from random girls on Tinder. It's every blokes dream fantasy. They are all jealous of you."

With that we walked outside and I walked her up to her car. I hesitated as to whether to give her a kiss. And then I wondered if it should be on the lips or just on the cheek. I really am well out of my depth in these situations. She settled the argument for me. She leaned forward and gave me a kiss on the lips. Not just a passionate kiss. It was more of a hint that there might be more. I guess you had to be there.

With that she got into her car and drove off. I was left just waving at her for a few seconds. I really am out of my depth in this one!

I went home and thought of all of the reasons why this would not be a good idea. Then I thought of all the reasons why I thought this could be a good idea. I fell asleep and had a dream. It involved Janet but every so often it would turn out to be Bernie I was making love to. An odd kind of dream but also quite enjoyable!

Monday

I was in an absolutely great mood when I walked into the station. The Sarge did notice but he put it down to me winning a close game yesterday. The weather was fine and sunny but it may get cooler in the afternoon.

The Sarge brought me my coffee and then the Boss arrived. We sat around as a group and discussed the happenings of the weekend. Tananga giving up the two guys who then confessed to Ronnie's shooting was the hot topic of the meeting. We were disappointed that we could not use the confession concerning Ronnie. Mike suggested we could get the Crown Prosecutor to attend when the two lads gave their confession again. It was a good idea if a little impractical. We said we would work on it. The Sarge gave out the jobs from the Squad room. I ended up with a commercial burglary.

After the meeting the Sarge asked if Bernie and I had a lovers' tiff. He was only jokingly referring to the fact that I had almost ignored her since she had arrived. I immediately wondered if he had a reason to ask such a personal question. My instant denial gave the Sarge reason to think about things and I could not help but feel we were under his radar so to speak! I had only been in the CIB room for a half hour and I had already blown it with the Sarge! That was a good start.

I then had a call from Shi Low who asked if I was available to call around this afternoon. The way he spoke, I probably had little alternative other than to agree, so I had an appointment to see Shi low at 2pm.

I went out to my commercial burglary and it was a typical small appliance burglary, although the burglars would have needed a decent sized truck to cart away all of the gear they nicked. I got the fingerprint lads out as it was a decent burglary with lots of stuff nicked. I also got the photographer out for the same reason. I would have a trawl through the Trade me site later in the week as I had discovered Trade me was a popular site for flicking off stolen items.

The Boss had a word with the Crown Prosecutor and he was happy to go up to the hospital and see the guys who had been handed over on Saturday. When he got there he judged that they were no longer under duress so he would take their statement under our supervision. That way he could argue in court as to the mental ability of the offenders. We had the confession on tape and we got the CP, once it had been transcribed onto paper, to go back up and get the two Black Power lads to sign off.

We now had done as much as we could with the Black Power lads so we arranged to get them transferred to our custody and for them to make their first appearance in Court. Then we would get them sent off to Waikeria to await their trial. I had an hour to kill so I went up to see Ronnie. He was doing fine. His wound was definitely feeling a lot better. He was quite happy with Tananga being in charge of his Mob and I deliberately kept him unadvised that we had fluked the capture of the two lads who had shot him. Also Ronnie wanted a smoke. He could go out to the gardens where he could smoke but he had a lot of thinking to do and for that he liked to have a fag to puff on. Being limited as to when he could smoke was not helping his thinking process. So he said. There were a couple of lads on door duty for Ronnie allowing visitors in. The nurse was always having a go at the lads on door duty. When they changed the guards she seemed almost upset to not have her favourite Mob member to argue with. Maybe there might have been something going on there?

While I had time I also went to see Tananga after phoning him from Ronnie's bedside. I did that so he could ask Ronnie any questions if he needed to. Tananga had it all in hand and he was keeping things ticking over while Ronnie was incapacitated.

Tananga had nothing to report from the weekend. Things seemed to be quiet on the Tohi front. I did pass on the Boss's concerns that Tohi might be planning something but Tananga was unconcerned. If Tohi tried anything he would handle it, but until he did Tananga's role was to just keep things ticking over.

I went back to the station and had lunch with the Sarge. He did ask if I had continued my run of luck with the girls from Tinder but I told him I had met with Julieana on Saturday and she had been a nonstarter for me. So that was the end of that. He did ask whether my golf lesson had been the reason I had won at the weekend. I told him I probably thought so but then he mentioned that my putting had let me down on Sunday's game and that should be a worry to me. I had not noticed my putting was bad but he seemed like I should be disappointed with it. I never really knew whether he was winding me up or not but I did resolve to get out on my little patch of grass at home and just check it out.

At 2pm I was walking up the stairs to see Shi Low. I was allowed access into the mahjong room and then welcomed into the Shi Low's office. As always I was offered a cup of tea poured by the hand of Shi Low and then we sat down and I waited for him to open the discussion.

It's an odd thing to think about, but in Shi Low's office I always felt I should be discussing important things here. It was not the place for any idle chatter.

Eventually he started, "Detective Sergeant I understand you took delivery of some people of the Black Power persuasion on Saturday. That must have been fortunate for you. I understand they had some news for you."

I was immediately on the back foot. I had never directly linked Shi Low and the two Black Power lads together. Now I had a feeling what the meeting was about.

"We were indeed fortunate to meet with those people."

I took a sip of my cup to indicate to Shi Low I was waiting for his next words.

"Those people were well?"

Again I did not quite know where this was going. "Those people have spent the last few days at the hospital having their cuts and bruises attended to, and also their wounds around their fingernails required attention. Anything they may have said while being tortured is possibly not allowed to be used as evidence."

"Hmm," said Shi Low. "On an unrelated matter, it is possible that some of their friends may have entered one of my people's shops. Perhaps they may have offered some form of protection in the upcoming gang war."

I had heard this from the Sarge last week. Now I knew it was true. I had wondered what happened to those lads. "I can only appreciate that would be an unwise thing to do. I understand you already have an organisation where you would listen to your people and any complaints they may have."

"Well done, Detective Sergeant. That was very well phrased. Yes they did come in to one of my people's businesses. They were quite persistent in their suggestions. Fortunately I, more correctly, my people were able to persuade them we did not require their protection."

"Did this negotiation between the two groups require some persuasion. Perhaps a finger or two was broken, obviously by accident."

"Detective Sergeant, there was no accidental breaking of any fingers. Any such occurrence would only have occurred if further negotiations proved unsuccessful. Would you like some more tea, Detective Sergeant."

I gratefully accepted the offer of more tea, while Shi Low was pouring the tea it gave me a chance to think.

"So I can take it that the members of the Black Power group were persuaded to not offer you further protection."

"Oh, Detective Sergeant, if only life could be that simple."

I was at a loss for words now. All I could come up with was," I had heard that you were involved with negotiations and they needed some further argument or discussion. If I may be so bold, you broke their fingers and you broke a couple of their fingers, each!" I had lost the use of nice and polite words to talk of the situation. I really needed to get back to that habit when I was having a discussion with Shi Low.

"If I may talk about something of a different nature, on the Friday evening I was driving to my home on Dansey Road. I believe your Detective Inspector also has a home in that area. I understand we are near neighbours, just three doors apart. Be that as it may, I was travelling along Pukehangi Road with my dear friend in the car when I noticed two motorcycle riders attempting to overtake me. I looked to my left and the rear passenger. I believe you would say the pillion passenger?"

I nodded my confirmation and I did not speak.

"Yes, thank you, the pillion passenger was aiming a gun at my door. I believe it was something that you might call a shotgun? It is a common misconception that a car would accelerate out of danger. I have been taught by lesser skilled people who I would still consider competent at their job. I merely touched the brakes in that situation. I should tell you that the Mercedes 500 has excellent brakes and within a second the motorcycle had passed by me yet had still managed to discharge the weapon. My windscreen was shattered as was my good friend in the passenger seat. I should add that windscreen suffered a lot more damage than did my colleague. The windscreen was quickly blown away by my speed. My colleague suffered some pellet wounds to his chest and the loss of a very well fitting suit by one of the top tailors in Auckland."

"Your friend is okay?"

"My colleague is fine but that is of little consequence. The second motorcycle got away but the man with the weapon was secured as his motorcycle crashed just a short way down the road. We also secured the rider or the driver of the motorcycle. They were treated for their wounds at the scene of the accident.

"Are they okay?"

"Perhaps you could tell me, Detective Sergeant, as they are now in your custody."

Now that really threw me. I took a sip of my tea as I slowly thought through the ramifications of Shi Low's last statement.

"But they looked like they had been, er... interrogated." I was trying to choose my words wisely but I was left with trying to make the best of a bad job. My mind was going over every angle. Why would the Black Power want to harm Shi Low? Was it because they had refused the BP offer of protection? Was it because the Chinese had callously broken their finger? No that should be plural. It was fingers! Was Shi Low in any danger because of his breaking of the fingers? Was he in danger because he had handed over the BP lads to the Mongrel mob and when they had turned him down, then to the law?

I apologised to Shi Low, "I must apologise to you. Also I should apologise to your colleague who was disturbed by the attempt on your life. I had no idea of your involvement on being the target of a hit by the Black Power Gang. Beyond that I really don't know what to say."

"Thank you, Detective Sergeant. Your kind words will mean a lot to my colleague. As for the Black Power leader. I have already been on the phone to him. I have suggested that should he try anything against one of my people, such action will involve rapid retribution. I do not believe we will hear more from him."

"I can only apologise again for your being involved with such dealings. Your people and the law have always got on very well and although we may not approve of your ways of dealing with such annoyances we value your friendship."

"Well done, Detective Sergeant. We may almost make a civilised person out of you. That was very well spoken." Shi Low was smiling at me. For him it was almost a grin. I'd still be happy with a smile from Shi Low and I did value his friendship.

I wandered back to the station, all the while my head was spinning with the thought of Shi Low being involved with the gang war.

When I got back the Sarge and the Boss were both going out of the room but they hung on to hear me speak.

What I said managed to blow them both away. I told them of my conversation with Shi Low and how he had initially been persuaded to deter the Black Power lads from insisting they had the best protection. Then I told them about the attempt on Shi Low on Pukehangi Road. When I mentioned that they had treated the motorcyclist at the scene they asked how the motorcyclists had been. That was when I was able to tell them we already had these lads in custody. Whatever they were doing was forgotten as they both sat and digested what I had just told them!

"How was Shi Low's mate?' asked the Sarge.

"Some pellets in his chest area and a good looking suit is ruined, made by one of the best tailors on Auckland, Shi Low said."

"And we already have these lads in our custody suite?" asked the Boss.

"Yes and we have a confession witnessed by the Crown Prosecutor. If they try and knock that out of court they will have to try and knock over the CP's reputation at the same time. It's looking pretty good!"

By now it was getting late in the afternoon so I took the opportunity to wander downstairs and have a word with the two prisoners handed over by Shi Low. I questioned them together, which was something I did not do very often.

I started by asking them about the attempt on Ronnie. They were still, happy may be the wrong word to use but it gets the meaning across, to fess up to the attempt on Ronnie. When I questioned them further they were initially reluctant to say anything about the attempt on Shi Low and who may have authorised the attempt.

I left the room and rang Shi Low. I asked him about the attempt on him. He believed I may have been mistaken. During our very pleasant cup of tea this afternoon he had not made any claim to have been attacked. Yes, his Mercedes was in for repair but he was thinking of upgrading the Mercedes anyway so he probably would never see it again. I was beginning to understand the message I was getting from Shi Low. What he had told me about being attacked was basically confidential. I worked out later that he and Tohi had probably agreed that it had not happened and that way they could move forward without any further retaliation. I wondered how the handing over of the two lads to the law would go down. The Sarge told me later that it was probably looked on as the cost of doing business in Rotorua. I went into to see the two lads and told them I may have made an error re the attack on Shi Low. They seemed very relieved to put that incident, if it ever happened, behind them.

I went back upstairs and told the Boss and the Sarge that the attack on Shi Low had never happened. That's when the Sarge mentioned it was looked on as the cost of doing business. The Boss made some comment about how Shi Low's mind worked. Whatever! I left the office and went home for my tea.

That night I may have spent some time on the art of seduction on the Internet. For me it was purely a form of research in the eventual scenario I may ever get Bernie into bed. I would definitely want her to be satisfied with my efforts. That reminded me. I was supposed to get another lesson on the art of seduction from Janet. Maybe I would ring her tomorrow and see if she was available.

Tuesday

Another brilliant day, weather wise and the Sarge was waiting for me to make my entrance to the station as he handed me my coffee. We sat down along with the Boss and everyone else in our CIB room and discussed progress. The best bit was that we had the two lads in custody who had confessed to having an attempt on Ronnie. There were other things to talk about but that was our personal feel good moment.

The Sarge handed out the jobs from the Squad room and I had nothing to do. I decided to go and see Ronnie at the hospital and then to go and see Tananga. Once I was away from the office I also rang Janet and made a time to go and see her this afternoon. Call me a bit sensitive if you want, but I didn't want the other people in the office to know I was going to see Janet.

Ronnie was champing at the bit to get out of hospital. He wanted a cigarette but he had to wait until the nurse said he could go and the doctor was due for his rounds. He was frustrated at being told when he could have a fag, by a women, the nurse, but as the Boss had said, blokes would do what they were told by a woman if she spoke with authority.

I left Ronnie waiting for the doctor to arrive and went to see Tananga having rung first. I got into see Tananga and had a chat and a cuppa with him. He reckoned Tohi was being very well behaved at the moment. For him that was a sign that trouble could be brewing but he was well aware that he was only holding the fort for Ronnie so he did not want to start anything. I mentioned to Tananga about Shi Low and he or one of his lieutenants had made the offer to Tananga to hand over the two lads from Saturday. He figured as much as he had heard of Shi

Low's reputation. He didn't know what Ronnie would have wanted to do with them and he couldn't be bothered hanging on to them for a few days until Ronnie got out of the hospital, so he had rung me to sort them out. I was appreciative and we had another crime stat with a plus for us on our side of the ledger.

I left Tananga and went back to the station. Bernie and I crossed paths on the walk in and other than a hurried. 'You're still on for tomorrow night' and a very positive 'Yes' in reply we did not speak further.

I had lunch with the Sarge and I filled in time until I slipped away to see Janet.

Janet, as usual was waiting for me in her motel room on Malfroy Road. She dressed very nicely so I assumed I would have to do the full seduction bit on her. A part of me was quite looking forward to trying out my technique. I had been coached by the experts on the You Tube channel. Maybe I could show Janet a thing or two.

She asked me to sit down first and then enquired if I was horny. An odd question but she did ask so I replied in the positive. Then she told me a few things that a woman may need. Such as security and a nice atmosphere and then she said something which rather shocked me. "A woman has to feel safe and secure and also that you are going to want to see her again. So sex is not necessarily always on the cards. So let's see how good you are at seduction."

I did my best but I was aware I was not doing the best for her. She reminded me what I was there for and I immediately got aroused so she sat down again until the feeling had passed for me. Then she let me have another try. Boy was I making so many mistakes. She tried to explain that sex may be the ultimate goal but first she had to feel wanted. After a few errors in judgement on my part we eventually got naked and I had to say I was certainly ready to do my part of the transaction. Then she told me about a variety of things I could or should do to make her not feel like something to bonk and then leave. She suggested I should make her feel welcome in her naked state and then she showed me where to touch her and my mind was so confused I was no longer in the mood, well I can definitely say I was not in a state for entry, as it were.

She told me that the majority of girls were not happy with how they look. If they had small breasts they wanted bigger and usually vice versa. If I was going with a girl with smaller breasts I should take time to show I appreciated her breasts. The same with the bum. If she was well endowed in the bum area or less well-endowed I should still take the time to appreciate the girl and all of her assets.

She stopped my efforts and then showed me what she liked. Now I was ready to perform my bit and we had sex and then cuddled for a while. This was what I like to call my half time interval, for obvious reasons. Then she insisted I repeat what I had done before with just a bit more feeling and affection.

Obviously I had forgotten everything she said once I had reached my peak, as it were.

She went over it again and then told me to try again.

She said I had always come to have sex with her so I had a false feeling of security. It was guaranteed if you like. Now I had to be the seducer it was a whole different kettle of fish. Not only did I have to make sure she was happy to have sex with me! I also had to check if she wanted me to have sex with her again!

I must have been there for over an hour and a half but it was one of the best sessions we had ever had. She thought it was among the top three. Her being pleasured was one of the reasons she enjoyed it so much. She reckoned I may need another lesson. Was I free on Thursday? She could fit me in at 2.00pm so I booked her in to my schedule. I left Janet's feeling pretty pleased with myself as I walked back to the car.

As I walked back to the car I turned my phone back on only to see I had received two calls from the office. Sitting in my car I rang the office and got put through to the Sarge. I enquired what was going on. His next words chilled me. "Tananga is dead. They got him on Clayton Road. Ronnie has said he is back in charge and he wants out of the hospital. The DI is up at the scene on Clayton Road and expects you up there. If you have been to see one of your girls for god's sake don't tell him. Just get your ass up there."

With that the Sarge rang off and I wanted to ask him so many more questions. When did it happen? How did Tohi get to Tananga? He was so careful, normally. How will Ronnie react?

All of this and much more was going through my head as I made my way up to Clayton Road. They had got Tananga as he slowed down for the road speed bumps in Clayton road. He had not been killed by a bullet but he had fallen off his bike as the impact of the bullet hit him.

I parked my car and walked up to where the DI, the Boss was talking to witnesses. He briefly acknowledged me and continued talking to the woman he was busy with. Evidently this woman had been following Tananga up Clayton Road when he had suddenly fallen off his bike and she had only narrowly avoided him. The Boss told me to not let anyone leave the scene and continued talking to witnesses. There were already two Squad cars on site and between them we managed to corral all of the witnesses together. The Boss eyeballed me as he walked past and I knew I would face an inquisition at some point. The ambulance had arrived but Tananga was already dead so it was a case of waiting for the ambo to take the body away to get the autopsy done. The Boss gave his permission so the ambulance drove Tananga away to the morgue. I was told by the Boss to make myself useful and see where the bullet that hit Tananga could have come from.

I wandered up and down the road and I found an ambush site around 100 yards up on the right hand side. It would not have taken a great marksman to hit Tananga when he was slowing down for the speed bumps. There was a church there and there would have been no locals to wonder what a guy carrying a rifle would have been up to. I cast around and found a shell casing. I bagged it and marked the spot with an evidence tag. Then I wandered down the road to the scene again and waited for the Boss to be free and I could report in.

The Boss listened to my report and then walked ahead of me to the site where the sniper had waited. I showed him the shell casing which would have been automatically ejected from the Rifle. He grunted something about wanting to see me in his office in the morning and walked back to the scene of the crime.

I also walked a few yards behind the Boss and he said I should go and see Ronnie at the hospital. If he had not been told I could tell Ronnie but I also had to tell him to stay on the hospital. If he was at the hospital they could put another few guards around him beyond his own lads. It would be easier to protect Ronnie at the hospital than it would be at the Gang HQ where we were inhibited by the lack of a police presence.

I went to the hospital but Ronnie had already gone. I rang the Gang HQ and was told Ronnie was there. I said I was on my way.

When I arrived at View Road I was not surprised to see the odd shotgun and rifle leaning against the upper levels of the outer perimeter. Along with a few gang members who were ready for anything that Tohi could organise against them.

I was let in after I demonstrated I was not carrying a weapon.. It's an odd feeling when you have to show you are unarmed in Rotorua but I could appreciate the Gang's caution.

I was allowed in and Ronnie met me inside the gate.

"This is bad, Sarge," was his opening remark.

He continued, "Tananga was only here because I was in hospital and now the bugger's dead and Tohi has to pay."

I was ever the copper trying to stop an escalation in the war. "We don't know if it was Tohi yet."

"Sarge, who else would it be?"

In the back of my mind I recall being grateful that I was considered a friend and above suspicion. I suppose from Ronnie's point of view you had to decide who was your friend and who was your enemy pretty quickly. I replied that I had no idea but let's keep things on an even keel for the moment I then suggested a brew would be good. Ronnie reluctantly agreed and led the way upstairs.

I made the brew as Ronnie's arm was still giving him pain. He was supposed to have stayed in for another couple of days but he had signed himself out because of what had happened to Tananga. I think the nurses were again secretly pleased to have the makings of a gang war now set away from the hospital. I sat with Ronnie for a good half hour. His only aim was to make sure that Tohi paid for Tananga. There was lip service paid to the killing of a gang member of the Mongrel Mob but I could see Ronnie was taking it personally about Tananga.

I left Ronnie wondering how he was going to tell Tananga's partner about his death and I went back to the station.

The Boss had been out to see Tohi who had of course denied anything to do with the killing. The Boss was still convinced that it had been under Tohi's explicit instructions.

It was too late to expect anything from Mike at the morgue so I knew I would have to wait until tomorrow. I already knew it was basically a bullet to the chest that had killed him and anything after that was superfluous to his death.

I asked the Boss if he wanted to see me today but he reckoned he was way too pissed off at me to even think about saying anything today. It was after five o'clock so I went home and wondered what I would be in for when we did have our little chat in the morning.

<u>Wednesday</u>

I was oddly resigned to the fact that I would get a bollocking today. I rather hoped the Boss would not be aware I had been visiting with Janet but if did he make that assumption, then so be it.

I walked in at my usual time and the Sarge was making a coffee when he saw me arrive.

"I thought you might have been later in today, what with you getting a bollocking from the Boss, today."

"If I get a bollocking I deserve it. Although there is no way I could have known what Tohi was up to." Just then the Boss walked into the office. He saw I had my coffee in my hand so he motioned me to follow him into his office.

I walked and did not sit down. If I was to get a bollocking I should stand up to get it.

The Boss simply said. "Well, sit down, then."

When I sat down the Boss apologised for being short with me yesterday. There was no way I could have known about what Tohi was planning. If anything he should have picked up that Tohi was planning a big move, but he didn't. He reckoned his NLP should have made him enquire further.

I did ask him what NLP was. He reckoned it was something called neural linguistic planning. It was something that you should know about if you had done the BA in Criminology like he had done. Evidently it was where you looked when you thought about something for a moment. It gave you a clue as to whether the guy was telling porkies or was inventing something you wanted to hear instead of what was really being planned.

Having said that, he gave me a sort of roasting over the coals for visiting with one of my 'criminal informants' and turning my phone off. If I was on duty I should always be reachable. He knew where I had been and although he did not usually object, he objected when I turned my phone off. As for me I reckoned I got off lightly and it was probably inappropriate to tell him I was having a sex lesson from Janet in order for me to be better in bed with another of his CIB team. Yeah, better left not spoken about!

I didn't see Bernie at all that day and I was hoping I would so I could check she was still on for this evening. Yes I am a little insecure about myself. I had nothing on my plate for today as the Sarge had handed out the jobs to whoever was available while I had been in the Boss's office getting a mild rollicking.

I went up to see Ronnie but I had left it until the middle of the morning. When I got up to Ronnie's I was surprised at the activity. There were all sorts of things going on, Yes, the mob members were still manning the fortress and I was allowed in without being checked for a weapon. I assumed they would know by now I was never armed unless I was required for an AOS callout.

Tananga was going home in style. The local chapter were going to escort the hearse as far as Tirau. Then each local chapter would escort the hearse through their patch, whatever they called it. I was surprised at how many chapters there were. Tirau, then Hamilton and then there were another four chapters who would ensure the hearse had a peaceful drive all the way up to the funeral home in Glen Eden. He would lie in the funeral home for a couple of days and then be buried with at least a dozen or more chapters in attendance. Don't get me wrong. I liked Tananga but I was still pleased to see him honoured by his peers. He deserved the recognition for the way he had acted when Ronnie was 'incapacitated' by the drugs and such like.

I was enjoying a brew with Ronnie and he was telling me how he would be looking for revenge once the funeral was over, when I heard the noise of engines, motorcycle engines outside. Suddenly everything changed In the room. One of the Mob members came dashing to whisper in Ronnie's ear. Ronnie looked at me and said," Tohi is outside with his gang. Time for us take a shot at him, the bastard." With that he sped away. I followed Ronnie out but I couldn't see him at first. Someone pointed Ronnie out to me. He was struggling to get up the outside stairs up to the upper level and then he was trying to get a shotgun up to his shoulder. His wrong shoulder, as I knew Ronnie was a left hander. I shouted at Ronnie to get his attention. It might have taken two or three seconds for Ronnie to turn around to me. It seemed like minutes rather than seconds.

I shouted up at him that this was not the best way to handle this, but my efforts were wasted. This was the way he wanted it handled!

Now if you think about my position. I was in the middle of a standoff, completely unarmed, with two gangs facing off against each other and Ronnie was on god knows what morphine for his pain so was probably not in the best position to make any decisions.

I don't know what came over me but it seemed like a good idea at the time. It seemed like the best of ideas at that point!

I pushed my way forward and around the car blocking the gates. I opened the gate and moved forward to meet the other gang. I do remember turning around and pushing the gate closed. I vaguely remember hearing something being relocked behind and I walked up to the gang who were probably fifty meters away. I stopped after about forty meters and waited. Three riders gunned their engines and eased forward to meet me. I didn't know but I was still in effective shotgun range at forty meters. I was also blissfully unaware that both sides had weapons and most of them were pointed at me as the loony who had left the security of the fortress behind me.

One of the guys who came forward was Tohi. I had met him a week or so ago and or whatever reason I remembered him.

I said the first thing I could think of which was "Tohi".

He replied by saying, "And you are Detective Sarge. Colin Woods mate."

"Why are you here, Tohi?"

"To pay respects to a fallen comrade. Tananga may have been with the Mob but he was a good guy."

"And you guys are armed." I looked at the assembled Black Power lads on their bikes. "Armed to the bloody teeth, I would reckon."

"So are the Mob. Stupid to come here if you aren't armed."

His answers were short and to the point. I really don't know what kind of reception he expected. He may have wanted the confrontation for all I know. I held up my jacket to show I was not armed.

"Well I am not armed and I reckon there is any one of them up there who would fancy taking a crack at you right now. Why don't you all go home before there is a bloodbath on the road."

"Okay, Detective Sarge. You tell Ronnie we only came to pay our respects. Tell him it was sod all to do with us. You remember to tell him that!"

With that they slowly pushed back their bikes and reformed and then drove away. I watched them as they turned the corner and drove away until I could no longer hear their engines.

For me, I could now hear my heart beating. I slowly walked back to the front door of the Gang HQ and knocked on the door.

I'd like to think that I walked back inside with a nonchalant air. The reality was that I was virtually out on my feet with the tension. I had just put myself in the middle of a gang war with perhaps 70 gang members all armed to the teeth with their weapons pointed in my general direction.

Ronnie was the first to speak, "That might have been the bravest thing I have ever seen. Or it could be the most stupid. Maybe it was both!"

Then he shouted upstairs to get the Sarge a cuppa. Reckoned I might need it after that.

I was on the point of collapsing with exhaustion or something like that. I had been stupid but it was the only way to avoid a bloodbath and I would have been forever remembered as the guy who was inside the Mongrel mob HQ. I slowly drank my cup of tea and it was nearly finished before I managed to ask Ronnie, "So how is your day going?"

We laughed at my sheer bravado or stupidity but Ronnie did acknowledge I might have saved a blood bath from happening. I had a cuppa and I left the gang HQ. I definitely did not want to go back to the station. I needed some time to think. In the end I went back to the station. It's odd but when you have just done something stupid you need friends around you. At the moment I could only think of the Sarge or the Boss or Bernie. I realised that was a bit odd. I now counted Bernie as one of my friends. I went back to the station and walked inside. I somehow knew I should not mention this incident until I had time to think about it.

The Boss walked out to meet me and said something like, "Come on, you. Mike has the report ready for us" I assumed he meant the autopsy on Tananga but I was not really interested. I made some excuse and asked the Boss for the rest of the day off. I told him I was not feeling too well so he said that was fine and he walked off to the carpark and then drove to see Mike at the morgue.

I went home and sat down for a while. Yes I had been stupid but yes it was probably the smartest thing for me to have done. I was probably the only one that could have defused the situation with Tohi. I sat and thought about the whole situation for a while. Tohi was stupid to have done what he did. He should have known there could or would have been violence. I let it go that Tohi might have been merely there to acknowledge a fallen comrade. It was the easiest thing to do and I let my mind drift off for a while. Before I knew it I was asleep and I woke up with a start a little after 3.00. I must have needed it. And on the bright side I should have another date with Bernie this evening. Yes, I must have needed the short rest. Now I was feeling a bit more positive about myself. Yes, life is good.

Chapter 7

I headed up to the CT club on Moncur Drive. I had taken a little extra care in choosing my wardrobe. I was looking forward to seeing Bernie.

I might have been just a touch early but Bernie was already there and waiting for me and had already got the drinks in. She stood up and greeted me with a nice peck on the cheek.

We settled ourselves down and then she asked how my day had gone. I replied that I had taken a half day off as I was not feeling too well but knowing I was meeting her made me all better. It was my attempt at a little humor.

She then asked if anything had happened when I had been to see Ronnie, today. I somehow got the feeling that she already knew but I explained to her in vague detail what had had happened.

She went barmy on me. She had heard from the Boss, who came back from Tohi's place, all about my activities in View Road. First she went ape at me about how could I ever put myself in that position. Then it morphed into me being reckless, bordering on stupid. Then it turned into her not becoming too emotionally attached to me if I was looking for a hero's bloody death.

I thought that I was the only one who had decided that Bernie could be the best thing that had happened to me! She was about to launch into another tirade when I leaned forward and kissed her.

What can I say. It seemed like a good idea at the time?

She responded equally passionately and then pulled away saying, "No, that doesn't mean you are getting sex tonight. I'm still bloody mad at you." Then she kissed me again.

The CT Club is not a place where passion reigns supreme unless you are playing snooker or pool. For us, sitting in the lounge seats, it was also not something that was usually encouraged. We sat back and slowly sipped our drinks.

I muttered something about her not being overly emotionally attached.

She replied that she had always fancied me from the day she first met me. Evidently I had picked her up from the airport on Te Ngae Road and delivered her to the station so she could meet the people she would be working with. I had actually forgotten that part. Then I had taken her to her new flat on Pandora Avenue and dropped her off. I was my usual friendly self but she had seen just a bit more in our future. When she heard I had been trying Tinder out she thought she may have lost her chance but then her mate had suggested she also try Tinder and see if I landed on her page. Evidently there were more tricks to try if that didn't work.

"So where does that leave us now?" I enquired.

"I don't want to jinx anything, so I suggest we take it wherever it wants to go. Provided you are not some Rambo type of guy, I reckon this might have a chance."

I gave her a peck on the cheek and asked, "Can I buy you a drink, little girl?"

She replied, "Yeah, but there's still no chance of sex tonight."

I replied, "I wouldn't want it any other way."

With that I walked over to the bar. Her temper I had survived and she did show a fiery temper when she went on to me about being a hero with a death wish. I looked back at her as I waited for my turn to be served. She was a very attractive woman. Then she caught me looking at her so I turned back to the bar. Self-consciously I may have sucked in the makings of my very small beer belly. It's a guy thing!

We had an amazing evening and the topics ranged from other people at the cop shop, her ex-husband and how he now wanted to get back with her. The lack of kids, his choice, and latterly her choice when she decided a career in the Police was her best option. We also discussed people she had interviewed and how she sometimes struggles with her interview technique. I told her she should be asking the Boss to improve her techniques at interviewing as he had helped me tremendously.

I don't know what other topics we covered but Bernie was an easy person to talk with. I enjoyed the evening and I got the same result as I kissed her good night. There was the promise of something a little extra. We had arranged that she would cook me dinner on the Saturday night rather than meeting again at the CT Club. I wondered if there might be anything else on the cards but I did not want to make any assumptions. I really liked Bernie and I did not want to assume anything.

I went home and had an early night. Life was good when you sorted your priorities out.

Thursday

I walked into the station and was met with my usual cup of coffee by the Sarge. He handed it to me and then said the Boss was looking for me to give me a bollocking and then he said, "And here he is, right behind you. Good luck."

The Boss walked in behind me and said, "Finish your coffee and then I will see you in my office. You are allowed to have someone in with you but I don't reckon you want anyone to hear what I have to say. But it's your choice."

I got up and started to walk to the Boss's office when he stopped me, "I said finish your coffee first and then I will do the bollocking. What? I'll see you in five minutes." With that he walked into his office and closed the door.

It must have been around five minutes later when I knocked on his office door. He barked at me to enter and then told me to sit down. Then he gave me the dressing down of my career in the Police.

"Tohi told me what happened yesterday. He reckoned it was one of the bravest things he's ever seen. For me I'll say it was probably the most stupid thing I have ever heard of as a DI. No, make that in my whole career with the Police. Whatever possessed you to do something that stupid!"

I mumbled something which was to the effect that it seemed like a good idea at the time.

I said something about not feeling particularly brave and he responded with. "Well, That's great. At least Ronnie and I can agree it was stupid."

I said he was not the first person to say that to me. I was thinking about what Bernie had said last night. He responded, "Oh so someone else reckoned you were being stupid as well. Who was that?"

I was now trying to think, "Er Ronnie reckoned it was either brave or stupid and he was going with stupid."

"So Ronnie and I agree on something at last. What the hell were you thinking? Did you reckon I would have to get up at your bloody funeral and say nice things about you? Did you fancy having a plaque on the wall with your photo on it? In memory of a fallen comrade. Ronnie was right it was bloody stupid and the only reason I won't put you up for an award for bravery is because I reckon you are too bloody stupid to know when to worry."

He slowed down and started to breathe normally again. His voice at last became a little quieter as he said, "Mark what you did yesterday was bloody stupid. If you have a death wish do it on your own time. Till then I want a DS I can rely on. Do I make myself clear?"

"Yes, Boss." With that he told me to get out of his office. I walked out of the office and straight to my car. I drove away until I could think. I believe I was down at the lakefront at the back of Tudor Towers before I finally had a chance to get my head in order.

I sat and thought for a half hour and then I went back to the station and walked back into the Boss's office and apologised for being stupid. The Boss now had it out of his system and he grinned at me.

"It had to be said, Mark, and I am glad I said it. Now get out of my office and do something useful."

The Sarge had been a little concerned about me heading in to see the Boss and then when I walked straight out and into my car he was more concerned. He couldn't hear what the Boss was talking about but he knew it was a bollocking and I was on the receiving end of it. He had handed out the duties to everyone else in the room, including Bernie, and he had then waited and hoped I would come back to the station.

He did enquire how I had got on with the Boss. All I could say was that the Boss had been dead right and I deserved a bollocking for doing something stupid. Whether he knew what it was about or not, he just nodded his head and went on his way.

I was busy doing something related to the death of Tananga. It might have been allowing the Mob members to escort the hearse back to Glen Eden. I spent the next hour on the phone speaking to each division on the route. I didn't want there to be any hiccups on the way. Tananga deserved better than that.

I had myself hunched over my computer. It was nothing deliberate but the Sarge respected I needed to be on my own and left me that way.

It must have been just after 12.00 when I realised I had not been given the morgue report on Tananga. I looked it up on the files but it had not made it that far. I wandered into see the Boss and he fished it out of a pile of paperwork and flicked it open.

"Tanahanga Eru Morton. Born blah blah. Died blah blah. Here it is. Suffered a bullet wound to the upper right quadrant of the chest area resulting in him being probably temporarily unconscious and resulting in him falling from his bike. Death due to the bullet wound which was .357. That's someone going for big game! And then, as a result of his neck being broken at the severing of the cartilage between the third and fourth cervical vertebrae, probably dead within a second or two of being hit by the bullet. At least it was a quick way of dying. Here add this to the file. Have you spoken to the Divisions along the route yet?"

"Yeah, I just spent the last hour on the phone to them. Good to hear he died quickly." Even though he may have been a patched gang member it was still a good way to go if you had to go.

I returned to my desk. I was glad the Boss had felt for me enough to give me a roasting. We definitely don't need heroes in the Police. You do want to be seeing your colleagues again, the next day. What I had done was brave but it was also stupid. Moving on I went to the Sarge who also gave me a mini roasting for being stupid. He knew the Boss had already given me a roasting but he also wanted me to know that he was also concerned for my welfare. He mentioned, in his roasting, about the nice birds on Tinder and I definitely did not want to miss out on those girls, did I? Oh, Sarge. If only you knew!

I don't know why but I suddenly thought of Janet and it reminded me I had a lesson from her that afternoon. I was alert to the fact that I needed coaching in the art of seduction and she was a very patient teacher. Also I had really enjoyed the last lesson from her. What time was it, now? Just after midday and I was due to see Janet at 2.00. I returned to my desk and busied myself with paperwork until 1.00. I had my lunch on my own and I returned to my desk and continued with paperwork until a little before 2.00.

I arrived at Janet's on time and she was waiting for me and nicely dressed in the dress she had worn for the swingers' party. I rather hoped she would have on the very nice underwear she had worn for that particular occasion. I assumed I would have to try out my seduction techniques if I wanted to get that far.

She greeted me warmly and told me to try my best. If I got as far as getting her naked she would give me marks out of 10.

I did my best and I did get her to the point of lying on the bed and without anything on. She did have the nice underwear on and I removed the panties with my teeth. Guys, it's not worth the effort! But she seemed to appreciate it.

She gave me 7 out of 10 for up to that point. Now she was naked I was undeterred by the need to be seductive. I got marked down to a 3 out of 10 for that bit. I really had to concentrate on pleasing the woman. I got a 9 out of 10 for doing the deal or whatever you want to call it. At the half time interval she told me what I had done well and where I had lost points with her. Basically, I should always remember there were two people in this transaction and both had to be happy with the interchange. I tried again and she insisted she should be clothed again so I lay on the bed while she got dressed again. That might have been an error of judgement on my part but I did manage to calm myself down.

Overall I got a mark of 8 out of 10 for my second performance but I did have to remember there were two people who were looking for enjoyment and not just me. We did have a chat at the end while were both naked and she said she would miss not having me as a regular visitor. I tried to say she was wrong but she reckoned I would only be calling if I never found a regular bird on Tinder. Why would I want to visit her anyway if I was getting it regularly from my girlfriend? I had not actually thought about that side of the relationship. Also the girlfriend would not want me to be seeing a hooker if she was happy to provide for my needs. Why was life so damned complicated!

I went back to the office and carried on with my paperwork. Today was the day that Tananga's body was to be escorted back to Auckland. Despite all advice to the contrary, Ronnie was determined to ride in a car ahead of his motorcycle escort as far as Tirau. At Tirau they handed over Tananga's remains in the hearse to the local chapter. Then they waited until the cortege left Tirau before heading back to Rotorua. I went round to See Ronnie when he returned and I had finished being given a lesson by Janet.

Ronnie was very pleased. Rather than a sedate twenty or thirty KPH procession they had acknowledged Tananga's love for speed and the procession had an average speed of around 100 KPH. I agreed that Tananga would have appreciated that.

Ronnie was just a little down at the passing of what had been a good friendship and I also reminded him that Tohi had insisted they had sod all to do with Tananga's death. Ronnie reckoned he was still wondering about that. I left him thinking about it and I went home.

All in all I had a good day. The Boss had given me a bollocking for being a hero, as had Bernie. I had my second lesson from Janet and I had scored an 8 out of 10 with my repeat performance once she had reminded me of what I was supposed to do. Lastly I had gone to see Ronnie. He was not convinced about Tohi's involvement with Tananga's death but he did seem to be prepared to weigh up the evidence.

All In all a good day.

Friday

Everything was back to normal in the CIB room. Mike and Bernie and also Derek were in. I ended up with a case of a retail burglary on Hinemoa Street. I walked around to the site of the offence. A jewelers and souvenir shop. It was an odd situation as they mostly stocked souvenir type stuff for the tourist trade. I figured they didn't have that much local trade as their prices were more suited to the tourist looking for a good quality souvenir. I went through the usual questions and got the fingerprint lads in to do their thing. I also took a few pics on my phone. It wasn't something I expected to get a good result from as I figured a lot of the items nicked would already be on their way to Auckland to be fenced there. The tourists were less picky in Auckland, and they would be happy to pick up a souvenir from Rotorua without ever having gone there.

Another thing occurred to me. I had heard nothing of my rapist for a few weeks. I should be hearing something from him by now. Three weeks was a long time between sexual assaults. I mentally prepared myself for getting a disturbed night's sleep and wondered whether I should give Tim Cross a ring when he woke up. Surely he would not have dealt with a sex assault by himself?

I went back to the station and had a cuppa with the Sarge. He did ask me how I was going on with the birds from Tinder. I said a gentlemen never tells on his love life so he automatically assumed I had not been successful for the last couple of weeks.

I went up to see Ronnie and he quizzed me on why I reckoned Tohi was telling the truth for a change. I said I had nothing to add but it was just a gut feeling. I also reckoned the Boss thought Tohi was lying through his teeth but neither of us had anything we could prove, either way.

I left Ronnie who said he would be up in Auckland for Tananga's funeral on the Monday. Ronnie was still pissed off that he would not be able to ride a bike at the funeral. He was really still confined to travelling in a car as the surgeons had had to virtually re-break his arm to get to all of the source of infection in Ronnie's arm. I wondered whether I should go as I had relied heavily on Tananga to stand in for Ronnie when he was high on the mixing of drugs. I decided I should not go and told Ronnie accordingly. Ronnie reckoned he would say something at the funeral and he would say something for me as well.

After lunch I went back to the office and it was quiet. The Boss was doing some paperwork, as was the Sarge. The other three were also doing paperwork. If you like it was all very calm. I wondered if it might be the calm before the storm but I did mention it to the Sarge and he told me it might also be a sign that the gang war was over. Stranger things had happened before and he remembered the last time in 05' when the war just stopped as if the gangs had seen enough of war and just wanted to get back to business. No-one had bothered mentioning this to the Police and for another couple of weeks they were wondering what was going to happen next.

I continued on with paperwork until around 5.00pm and then went home for a quiet night.

I may have gone on to some the sites that mentioned seduction. I was still a little uncertain how things would happen if she did this or that. I wanted to be ready for anything and it didn't do me any harm giving myself a refresher course.

Saturday

I had a lie in on the Saturday. It might have been around 9.30am when I got up. I had a whole eight or so hours before I was expected at Bernie's. I had determined I would have a shower just before going to see Bernie. Just in case, well you never know?

I got dressed into my scruffy gear and went out on the lawn to practice my putting. I figured the grass would need mowing before I practiced my putting so I went back inside and never bothered. I surprised myself once I realised I was quite nervous about this evening. I tried to analyse why, but I just wanted this evening to go well. I knew I liked Bernie and that just added that little bit more pressure.

At 7.00pm I was sat outside Bernie's doing a personal check. Showered, shaved, bit of smell nice on and a bit down there just in case. Wine, a reasonable bottle of good stuff, well it was $40 a bottle so it can't be that bad, and a bunch of flowers for good measure. It dawned on me that she reckoned she did not drink. I'd play that one by ear, but I must remember not to drink the bottle of wine myself. One I would not be able to drive and secondly I may not be able to perform.

Yep, I had done as much as I could, so I knocked on her door.

She greeted me with a kiss so that was good start. She then wandered back to the stove suggesting, over her shoulder, that I should put the flowers in water and then she told me where the wine glasses were.

I quite liked her place. Given it was quite minimal I figured she would be of a tidy mind and the like. I preferred that in a woman.

We sat down to dinner and she had cooked a roast lamb. It was delicious and then we had something for a dessert. Perhaps apple pie and ice cream. Whatever it was it was great and I wondered whether the subject of sex would come up tonight.

We settled our dinner down with another glass of wine. I queried that she said she didn't drink when I had taken her out before. She told me it was probably some kind of Dutch Courage. I hadn't heard the expression before.

"You Know Dutch Courage. When you have a drink first, to er... get you. You Know."

I said I didn't know what she was on about, so she stood up and said, "I'm in the mood for sex, I hope you are as well." With that she remained standing and holding out her hand for me. I stood up and she led me to the bedroom.

I was busy trying to remember everything that Janet had told me about being a seducer. It was not needed as Bernie proceeded to strip off and jump into bed.

I said something which was not my proudest moment in my career of being the great seducer, "Well, that takes away the issue of consent!"

She looked at me and then said, "For god's sake, get in. it's cold with nothing but these sheets on."

I hurriedly stripped off and jumped into bed alongside her.

Can I say she was an active participant. No, I'll say she was an enthusiastic participant. I forgot all about what Janet had told me as I tried to keep up with her. She was a leader and I really don't want to go into all of the details but we had a lot of fun and she repeated that she fancied me since the first day we had met at the airport.

Yes, we managed to get through twice, you know what I mean, so move on. And, we cuddled at the half time interval and then again afterwards. I wanted to be honest so I told her that I had never thought of her as a woman since we had first met. It's all part of the PC culture we have to endure with the new gender discrimination laws. Now I most definitely regarded her as a female and a damn sexy one at that.

She wanted me to go home after we had sex or made love or whatever it was. She needed to be alone with her thoughts. We arranged to meet on the Wednesday evening again, at the CT club. To be honest I probably needed some time to think about things as well. I had never been quite so smitten with a girl before. I needed to do some thinking, as well.

We kissed while she was still in her dressing gown and I had got dressed. I went home and thought about what my love life now looked like. For the first time in twenty plus years, I had a love in my life and that was something new to me. This might sound stupid but after a while I figured I was okay with having a love interest in my life. With that I drifted off to sleep.

Sunday

I had the regular golf game with the Sarge and the Boss. The Boss and I were tied for first and the Sarge was a couple of shots behind us. He paid for the beer but the Boss had fluked a wedge shot at the eighteenth which went in. I had to struggle to match his score which I did and the Sarge was left ruing the chance at squaring the game by three putting.

Naturally the subject of my love life came up while we were having a beer, upstairs. I so desperately wanted to tell them about this girl I had met through Tinder but I kept my mouth shut so the Boss and the Sarge both assumed I was not getting that lucky on Tinder. I was happy to let them think that way. After the game I went home and thought I was lucky to get a chance at meeting someone at my age. If you are a bloke in your middle forties, you know what I mean!

Monday

In at my usual time and it was another lovely day. I breezed in and got my coffee from the Sarge. Bernie walked in at the same time as I and I was happy that I treated her exactly the same as the others in the room. We would have no problems hiding it from the team, until we decided we were after something more. Then it occurred to me that I wouldn't be happy if we broke up. Then I started to worry about a breakup. Call it just me being insecure, but I actually wondered how I would handle that. It wasn't a happy moment for me. I was invested in this relationship but how far should I push it? I tried to make the thoughts go away and I did succeed for a while and then I forgot about it all when the Boss called me into his office.

I sat down and the Boss looked at me for a few seconds.

The Boss started with, "I'm watching the 'Scrubs' Video at home. It's something that her indoors bought when she was at the Warehouse one day. In it there is one character called Cox who keeps going on a rant with one of his doctors about the sweet sex this young doctor is having with one of his co-doctors. I had a speech prepared worthy of this Cox bloke about you and a coworker having sex. It was a good speech. After you denying you were getting sex from one of your Tinder girls yesterday at the golf course and then watching you this morning almost ignoring Bernie, I'd like to ask you a question. Are you bonking Bernie? There's probably a nicer way of asking but you know what I mean!"

Yeah, he caught me on the back foot. "I, er, and what does that have to do with you?"

"It has everything to do with me. First off I am your Boss. Secondly, if I ever think you are giving Bernie any preference when you hand out the work in the morning, I have to be mindful. Thirdly, well some of the stuff you hand out can be dangerous. Again, I can't stand by and let you keep her out of danger. Now, again. Are you bonking Bernie?"

I had to admit he did have a good reason for asking, "Yes."

At the back of my mind I was thinking it had only been the one time or two times. Did that really count?

"Okay" the Boss replied. "From now on I might suggest to the Sarge that he gives out the work from the Squad room. Also I may step in if I reckon you are giving Bernie the better cases. After that I don't know what I'll do. I've never had anyone fraternize with a fellow officer before. It might be because we have only had blokes here before but that's by the by. Just be aware that you could be in a tricky position when the others find out. Oh and by the way, good luck, I reckon you and Bernie make a good couple. Anything else? Are you going to tell the Sarge or will you let me do that?"

"Thanks but it will sound better coming from me."

"Well off you go then. Go and do something with your day." With that I was dismissed. How did the Boss pick it up so damn quickly? I wondered to myself and then went out to see the Sarge. He was in a deep conversation with Mike. Bernie had already gone out on to see the case which had fallen on her watch. I sat down and waited for the Sarge to be free of Mike and his conversation.

I sat down with the Sarge in my little cubicle and explained what had happened and how Bernie and I had ended up as a couple. The Sarge reckoned we made a great couple and with shared interests and if I didn't say something stupid he could see a future for us. He then reckoned Huia, his wife, would be pissed off as she already had a couple of girls lined up for me to have dinner with.

I wanted to be away from the office so I went up to see Ronnie. That was no good as Ronnie was in Auckland and attending the funeral for Tananga. I thought about going to see one of my CI's but that would probably have involved sex and I was really wondering if I should be totally loyal to Bernie. Well, obviously that was a yes. So how did that translate when I rang one of my girls up? It became very complicated very quickly. I went down to the lake front and got myself an ice cream. I just needed time to think things out.

Loyal to Bernie? Obviously that was a yes.

What about my job as head of the Vice squad? I still had the three girls as my confidential informants. Is there anyone else that the Boss could insert into my job? Bernie was the next highest ranking officer in the CIB squad. That would not be a starter. It really needed someone with the rank of DS or higher to take on that job. Was that the Boss's problem or would he make it one of mine?

Could I see my relationship with Bernie going further? I wanted to think so but then my old doubts started to surface again. I couldn't shake them so I went back to the station.

On the drive back I realised I had no control over Bernie so I should just be as nice as I could to her and whatever happened would happen. I realised I would be doing that anyway so continued on my way to the station.

When I got back Tim Cross had called in and was busy regaling the Sarge and Bernie with some of the tales from his work as a security guard. A recent star on a tour had asked a girl to come up to his hotel room. When she had come up to the room Tim had figured the girl was too young to be in the room and had asked her for her ID. When she failed the simple test, Tim had turned her away and got one of the girls from Alexanders to come across. The star had been very well pleasured and had left Tim a generous tip. So Tim could now add being a pimp to his CV.

I had a quick word with Bernie and told her that the Boss knew about her and me. She took that as just one of the hassles of having a love life and was not too concerned. She confirmed our time for Wednesday evening and went out on another callout.

It was lunchtime and the Sarge and I had lunch. Given the topic of our most recent conversation it was awkward to not start anything with, 'So how is your love life." We coped but it was just a little awkward for a while.

I filled in my day going over paperwork and filing reports on Crime Stats etc. At 5.00 I went home and before I had got my foot in the front door I had a phone call from the Boss. "Shi Low is dead. There's been a car accident but it sounds iffy. Meet me at the corner of Sunset and Pukehangi."

With that he rang off and I turned back to my car and headed off to the scene. I reviewed the Boss's conversation in my mind. Shi Low was dead. That made me feel a little sad. I quite liked Shi Low even if he did represent a people he was the ruler of. Somehow I always felt on my guard with him but he did give me marks for trying to be like a 'civilised person'. I would miss my chats with him.

I arrived at the scene and parked my car off to the side. The Boss's motor was right at the scene. There were a couple of Squad cars there, an ambulance and a fire engine which was busy trying to get the body of Shi Low out of his car which was upside down in the middle of the road. He had already been pronounced dead and the fire engine was trying to extricate the body without doing too much further damage. I assumed that was so Mike at the morgue would be able to work his magic.

The Boss took me on one side, "The car will go off to the wreckers but I want a police guard on it until our forensics have had a chance to work on it. As far as I can tell he pulled up to stop at the stop sign and then accelerated to turn right to go home. He knew this road so there is no reason why he would have flipped the car over and why did he suddenly accelerate so quickly? Oh, yeah, the engine was racing when it flipped over. He knew the road so was he trying to get out of the way of something?"

I was trying to look at the whole scene, the bigger picture, if you like, "Why is he half turned to the right? His windscreen is back on the road and there doesn't look like a bullet went through it. You're right Boss, it does look iffy."

The wreckers' vehicle was backing up to the crime scene and the Boss was busy taking photos. Shi Low had been removed and taken away by ambulance to the morgue. The fire engine was waiting for the vehicle to be removed and then they would sweep the scene to make it safe for other traffic. Already there had been diversions put in place so were not getting hassled with other vehicles coming up to the stop sign.

The Boss and I walked through the scene. He pulled up at the end of Sunset and there were no signs of an issue. The Boss and I continued to follow the path of Shi Low's brand new Mercedes. We stopped every ten paces or so. About twenty or thirty meters in we found what could have been a bullet mark on the road. After which Shi Low would have started to take evasive action. By working back from the purported bullet mark on the road we could then tell when his car had flipped over and he had been killed.

The Boss told one of the squad cars to escort the vehicle back to the wreckers' yard and to stand a guard over the vehicle until further notice. After being at the scene for a good hour and a half, we felt we had done as much as we could and we went to our separate homes. On the good side, the accident to Shi Low had virtually wiped out the words I had had with the Boss this morning, right out of my head.

Unfortunately Bernie had been ringing my land line for an hour wanting to see how I was etc. She had assumed I did not want to speak to her so had stopped ringing.

I settled down to a fish and chip takeaway meal and watched the box for a few hours before heading to bed.

Tuesday

On Tuesday I was in at my usual time and the Sarge had my coffee waiting for me. It was another lovely day but I was still a little down at seeing Shi Low who I had considered a friend, of sorts, lying dead the previous night.

Bernie had collared me in the car park. She said she had phoned me last night but I hadn't answered so she left it. I told her about how I had ended up at the scene of Shi Low's accident. Then I had to tell her about Shi Low being dead. She wondered how that would play out and I told her I would keep her informed. To a degree it got me back to wondering how I would handle it if Bernie left and before I knew it I was in that sort of mood and walking into see the Sarge waiting for me with my coffee. The Boss had rung the Sarge and told him about

Shi Low last night. That meant I had one thing less on my plate so I waited for the Boss arrive. Fortunately the Boss had mentioned to the Sarge that it was now his job to give out the cases from the Squad room. I ended up with a domestic burglary and I went off to see about that situation. The burglary was a bit iffy. It might have been an inside job so I got the fingerprint lads out to do their thing and I would get back to the scene later.

The Boss had been up at the wreckers' yard along with the forensics team. They had worried at the wrecked Mercedes until they found what they were looking for. The front right tyre had a puncture wound and a wrestle with the car jack from the Mercedes meant they could determine that the bullet was still in the tyre and eventually they managed to separate the bullet and do forensics on it. Unfortunately there was not a lot that the bullet could tell them. It had been well worn from its abrasion with the road and they could only guess at its caliber. They thought they were looking at a .303 or even a .357 but that was the best they could get from it. It was a heavy bullet so it probably had come from a rifle. There was nothing they could pick out from the actual bullet itself as it was too abraded.

The Boss and the forensics team had a discussion. I would say that the Boss wanted to know more of the details and the forensics team were more fascinated with the actual bullet and its eventual insertion into the tyre of the Merc.

I sat down with the Boss later in the morning and we had a good talk about what had possibly happened. We both were convinced that the bullet had been actually fired at the Mercedes tyre. The Boss wondered why they had not simply shot at the driver. I reckoned they would want it to look like an accident so that is what we went with. By retracing the path of the Mercedes and where we believed the car started to rollover we were able to get a rough idea of what had happened. The bullet had hit the tyre just before the bend of the road was complete. Shi Low had felt the steering go wobbly and tried to accelerate to get away from a possible assassination attempt or a kidnapping and within a few meters the tyre had deflated and the car had rolled. The Boss reckoned Shi Low had only had the car for three days. Perhaps he was not used to the vehicle's odd ways, although he had had a very similar vehicle previously. We went back up to Pukehangi Road and walked our way through the scene. Now we had all the possibilities in our hand we were reasonably able to determine what had happened. We were pretty right with our assumptions. Then we had a look further up the road on both sides. We eventually found the site where the shooter had set himself up. He had positioned himself with a good view of the bend. It was much better position to shoot from than from the spot where Ronnie had the attempt made on his life. It was probably around 60 meters further away from the bend and gave the shooter at least a full two seconds to aim and fire. This shooter knew what he was doing. With both of us casting around we eventually found the shell cartridge. It was a ,357 but not the same gun as we had seen used before. This was a centre fire rather than a rim fire action. It was second nature to me but I did have to explain it to the Boss. I won't bore you with the details but we were looking for a different gun than used on Tananga.

I had a call on my cell phone. It was from Ki San Wang who was the new boss of the Chinese people. Would I have time to call around for a cup of tea this afternoon. He was aware of the special relationship that Shi Low and I had and he would welcome the opportunity to further cement that relationship. We arranged that I would go around at 3.00pm. The Boss reckoned I should definitely go and keep in with the Chinese people. I was actually honoured that Ki San Wang had considered me sufficiently high on the totem pole to see me on his first day. If you understand the question of face, it means I was somebody important on the relative social scale. We went back to the station. This afternoon we would get the report from Mike at the morgue. I rather hoped we would not be surprised by anything that Mike had discovered.

I had my lunch and rang Ronnie again. He was still coming back from Auckland and would not be back until later in the evening. I mentioned the death of Shi Low and Ronnie instantly jumped to the conclusion that Tohi was involved. I let that one slide and rang off after listening to Ronnie's description of Tananga's funeral.

I carried on with paperwork until it was time for me to go and see Ki San Wang. I was trying to remember whether it was polite among Chinese people to bring a gift with you when first meeting some of Ki San Wang's importance. I figured I would not and if he did then I would be lower in his eyes. Somehow I was ok with that.

I walked up the stairs to see Ki San Wang and the door was opened for me before I reached the top step. I walked through the mahjong room and there was no one playing. Ki San Wang was already in the mahjong room and ushered me into his office.

He made me welcome and sat me down and already the tea was in the room. I studied him through my western eyes as no doubt he was studying me. He was quite a bit younger than Shi Low. I would estimate his age to be around 45 or 50. As I had no ready reference in aging people who were Chinese I had to be content with my guess. He was very smartly dressed in a business suit which was the way I usually saw Shi Low. I assumed his suit cost more than a month of my salary but I had little time to think more as he started speaking and welcomed me.

I offered my condolences on the passing of Shi Low. Ki San Wang was just a little dismissive. "In our culture we very much believe in the afterlife so I am satisfied he is already in a better place. Now I believe you would prefer milk with your tea?"

I accepted his offer and we sat down and talked.

He was the first to speak, "Detective Sergeant, I understand you have been back to the scene of the accident already. Is it possible you have found anything that you would wish to share with our community?"

"Yes and thank you for this opportunity. We believe it is entirely possible the crash may not have been an accident."

"You would assume that because of the cartridge or shell that you found?"

I was on instant alert. This guy obviously knew way more than he was letting on. "Yes and we also found what appears to be a puncture on one of the tires. We have put things together and that is one assumption we have come up with."

"Let me assure you, Detective Sergeant, until the funeral occurs we shall seek no retribution for this matter. I should also add the funeral will be on Monday. I have yet to determine where we will have the funeral as I fear there may well be a great number of people who would wish to be present. May I ask you, Detective Sergeant, will you be attending?"

"I would deem it an honour if I was to be invited." I had not actually decided whether I was going to attend the funeral. I figured I should but then the awkward question would arise if I was not invited as it would be a Chinese type of funeral, probably.

"Detective Sergeant, you will always be remembered as friend and counsellor to Shi Low. If I may include you, you will be asked to sit with the other members of his family. I would assume you have a dark suit?"

"Yes, I do."

"Then that is settled. I will include you when I notify everybody of this occasion, and it will be an occasion."

We talked for a further, possibly a half hour. I wanted to know what he was going to do about Shi Low's 'accident' but he declined to comment saying only that until Shi Low had been laid to rest they would not seek any retribution. I quite liked Ki San Wang. When he wanted he had quite a mischievous or fun attitude about him. We parted company and I thanked him for his welcome.

Walking back to the station I was in a good mood. Because Shi Low believed in the afterlife his associates already knew he was there. I walked back into the station and the Boss asked how I had got on. I told him I had been invited to the funeral and had been asked to wear a dark suit. The Boss already knew that most of the mourners would be in white as that was how they did things in China. I did get a lifting of the eyebrows when I said I had been asked to sit with the family.

The Boss reckoned that Shi Low had always liked me and considered me to be a friend that somehow always managed to even give bad news that sounded like it was good news. He had also been invited to attend but not as a friend of the family. He would go but he did not expect to take a part in the funeral.

With that it was close to five o'clock so the Boss told us all to get lost for the day. He had a couple of calls to make and he would then have an early night. The Sarge would, of course, be there until 5.00pm.

When I got home I made myself a brew and sat outside on the now longer grass. I wondered about cutting it when I heard the phone ring. It was Bernie. Nothing special to ring about, she just wanted a chat while she had a cuppa. Okay, we might have spoken for over an hour and I was waiting for her to invite me over but she didn't! Maybe she was waiting for me to invite her over to my place. She was easy to talk to and the hour or so just seemed to fly past. There was none of that lovey-dovey stuff that teens might go on with but it was nice to have someone who was on your side.

That night I had one of those dreams where you started off making love to someone you had never seen before and then it turned into a scary movie type of thing. Not nice but I did enjoy the first bit.

<u>Wednesday</u>

On Wednesday after my usual start I went up to see Ronnie. He was still living at the Gang HQ and his missus was spending a few nights up there when she could get a friendly babysitter.

I sat and listened to Ronnie's account of the funeral. That was how he wanted to go he said. People got up and said nice things about Tananga. There was a haka, lots of good music going on in the background and probably well over 300 bikes escorted the coffin to the crem. The widow was grateful she had been among so many friends at this time and Ronnie assured me the widow would be well taken care of until she decided to remarry or shack up with someone. That informality quite tickled me.

I don't really recall what happened to the rest of the day. It passed quickly enough and I was looking forward to my date with Bernie.

I was on time for the CT club and Bernie was already waiting for me. I offered to get the drinks in and she reckoned she would be just as happy going back to my place. So we went back to my place and I mentally reminded myself that I had replaced the sheets that day. I must have known or maybe I was just keen. We did end up in bed and it was good for me. I did spend just a little time being the seducer and I think Bernie enjoyed it! We spent a little time working out how we would handle it if it became common knowledge around the office. Then we concentrated on other things and that's the way the evening went.

<u>Thursday</u>

As usual I went up to see Ronnie and had a chat with him.

I asked Ronnie directly if he had anything planned as retribution for the death of Tananga. He said he was keeping things quiet as he was still not able to lead an attack on Tohi. Until he was able to ride a bike again he was hoping things would stay quiet. He didn't for a moment believe that Tohi had nothing to do with Tananga's death and he was just biding his time, unless Tohi made another strike against the Mongrel Mob. I asked him to hold off doing anything until at least after the funeral of Shi Low. He agreed but it was really still a case of him being ready to ride a motorbike again so he could do something as a leader.

There were only two cases from the Squad room so Derek and Bernie handled them. I had a chat with the Boss. Tohi was still denying he had anything to do with Tananga's death and he was now also denying he had anything to do with Shi Low's death. I had him marked down as having something to do with Shi Low's death but without any proof I could not really even interrogate him. Also, he was the Boss's sort of contact or mate.

I had a word with the Crown Prosecutor or I should say he called me. He indicated that he may need an expert witness in his case against the two hit men on Tananga. I was pleased to be able to do something for the guy as he had done so much for us over the years. I told him I was available for a debrief any time he wanted me. It always pays to keep in with the CP.

The Boss had a quiet word about how things were going with Bernie. Things were fine, I told him and he reckoned I was behaving myself in the office and not paying too much attention to her. He did wonder how soon it would be before the rest of the team noticed we were going out. A good detective should be aware of what was going on around them so he rather hoped it would not be too long before anyone commented. I reckoned I could wait for the comments to start and he wished me the best in that. We also had a bet that Mike would be the first one to make a comment. What can I say? I fancied Tim as the first one to notice. Well he had known me for a lot longer so I reckoned he would have an idea sooner. It was only a bet for $10. Obviously I took the bet!

I had a call from Ki San Wang, the new leader of the Chinese people in town. He asked me to be there just a little early so I could meet the interpreter and also get to my seat in an orderly manner. I was impressed that Ki San Wang had even bothered to attend to the detail of an interpreter for me but as the service was to be a mixed service of both Chinese and English he wanted to make sure that everyone got value from the service. That's not a good way to say it but you do know what I mean. The funeral was to be held at St Luke's Church as it was one of the few that could handle the crowd expected. Also Shi Low had occasionally been to the church. He had dabbled with Christianity but he still wanted to be a part of the traditional Chinese beliefs. The funeral was set down for three o'clock as the number three was heavily associated with being a good number in their superstition.

I said I would be there at least ten minutes prior and he suggested I get there at least a half hour early. Most, if not all of the Chinese community would be there and he also anticipated a good few members of the local community. He said he anticipated a crowd of between 300 and 500 if the weather was fine.

I hung up the phone and wondered at how a simple Chinese guy could gather such a large crowd. The Boss was walking past with the Sarge. Between them they told me that Shi Low had been in charge of the Chinese Community for over twenty years. He was well thought of and not just in the Chinese Community. The Chinese took their local responsibility very seriously and made significant contributions to the local community. Yep, the Boss reckoned it would be a big funeral.

That might I went home and Bernie called me. We chatted for an hour and I was pleased to be in a relationship with someone who had similar interests to me. I reminded her that we were on for Saturday night and she told me I should not expect sex on Saturday. She did explain why but I was quite happy to be told when I could have it and I suggested we should do something different. Perhaps go for a meal and then go and see a movie at the local cinema. Yep, she was up for that so we made a time and booked tickets for the movies. I am in a relationship and it feels fine!

Friday

It may feel odd but I was a little disturbed at having nothing to do. The Gang war was going nowhere and nothing seemed to be happening. My list of cases from the Squad room was now being handled by the Sarge and he was being his usual efficient self and also doing the follow up when a case was being handled in a way he was not comfortable with. I had nothing to do on the Gang war front and I had no developments on the Shi Low front. To say I was bored would be something I should not be saying but the Boss was also at the same stage. We decided to go out and view the scene of Shi Low's 'accident'. If nothing else it filled in a half hour. Then we went up to see Ronnie. Another cuppa later and we had filled in another hour. Ronnie was still in a little pain from trying to overuse his damaged arm. With him being a left hander he was having to do everything with the wrong hand and he was not the most patient person. We then went to see Tohi and spent an hour there. Tohi was all smiles when he saw the Boss but the smile slipped a little when he saw me walking into the Gang HQ on Vaughans Road. He greeted me warmly enough and we were offered a cuppa which we accepted. It's odd but the general perception is that the gangs are heavy drinkers but the reality is quite different. Most of them do not drink if they are going to be riding their hogs. We left Vaughans Road and went back to the station. On a personal level I had the feeling that Tohi had something to do with the deaths of Tananga and also Shi Low. I voiced my opinion to the Boss as he was driving back into town. He agreed but as we were trying to keep things on a low level until after Shi Low's funeral, we both decided it was best not to pursue the matter until possibly Tuesday of next week.

The Boss and I shut ourselves in our cubicle and office until 5.00pm rolled around. I spent my time looking up various things. I did discover some interesting things on ballistics from an American site. I discovered that a bullet fired at point blank range still has 'potential' and is still accelerating as it leaves the gun until it reaches terminal velocity at which point it starts to fall to the ground. Yeah, well I found it fascinating.

I also researched how Chinese funerals went, as opposed to English funerals. They are quite different in terms of the family wearing white to honour the dead. The coffin with Shi Low's body was to kept at the home of Shi Low so the relatives could show respect. This was called 'shou ling'. The actual funeral service was called 'fa yin'. It gets complicated but offerings of food indicate the passing of the spirit and the relationship they still have with the deceased. There was a lot more as you would expect from a culture many thousands of years older than Christianity but it all got a little complicated for me.

I brought up 5.00pm and beyond checking we were still on for a game on Sunday with the Sarge, I went home. Bernie did not ring and I felt just a little disappointed. Perhaps I am acting like a teenager but it is my love life and I don't have a lot of experience to call on.

Saturday

Another nice day but it looked like it could rain in the afternoon. I decided to mow the lawns, which I did. I then spent a half hour with my putter on the grass. I didn't know what the Sarge was on about so I made my lunch and then had a snooze which was unintentional. I woke up in plenty of time at 4.30 and carefully showered even though I knew we would probably not have sex tonight. It had rained during my snooze and it might still rain this evening. Bernie was still a young lady who I wanted to impress so made sure to put the smell nice on. I still regarded her as a young lady. I was middle aged; she was young if she was still under 40. It's odd how you define middle aged. When I was in my late twenties I reckoned anyone over the age of 30 was middle aged. Go figure!

I met her at the CT Club as they still have great meals and we had a drink with our meal and had a pleasant time. Obviously our conversation pretty much centered around work related topics but it was still an enjoyable meal. We then had a choice of what to watch at the cinema, either a murder mystery starring some no-name or a rom-com with Jake Gyllenhaal. We made our decision and went with the rom-com. We had a very pleasant evening and I dropped her off at her door with a very nice kiss and went home.

For a no sex date it was very enjoyable for me.

On the Sunday I won the golf by a couple of shots and the Sarge ended up paying for the beers again.

It was, overall, a very nice weekend.

Chapter 8

Monday

I was in a great mood when I walked into the station. The Sarge had my coffee ready and it was a fine day. I had my best dark suit on and as I turned around the Boss walked in and he had his dark suit on as well.

We had our usual sit down where we discussed the happenings of the previous week and what we had to do this week. Mike and Bernie were the two DC's on duty today as Derek was still pulling the weekend shift cover.

The Boss and I had left little on our plates as we were booked in for the funeral today. I went up to see Ronnie after ringing first. Over the weekend he had tried riding his bike again and had failed. He wasn't bothered but he did mention that Tohi would have to pay when he did manage to get back on his bike. I had a look at Ronnie's bike. It always looked immaculate, well it would when you have a few lads whose job is to make sure your bike is always well presented. I looked closely at the left side of the tank where the tank had been in contact with the kerb. I was impressed with the job that the painter had done. There was not a mark on the tank.

We went upstairs for our usual cuppa and I had a pleasant half hour chatting with Ronnie. He still had an eye on what Tohi may do but he reckoned the gang war had run its course. He was more concerned with getting back to his drug business. I reminded him that I really did not need to know about that side of life. He grinned and apologised for reminding me that was how the gangs made their money. I got the impression he wanted to do something about Tohi but he was a bit cagier about that than he had been with his drug deals.

I wandered back to the station. The Boss had been to see Tohi and he was a little more concerned. He reckoned Tohi was still planning something against Ronnie but he could not get an idea of what he was planning. As far as the Boss was concerned the gang war was still not over. For me that was a problem for tomorrow. Today I had the funeral to attend. In a way I was looking forward to paying my respects to Shi Low. Also I was keen to see how a Chinese funeral would differ from a normal funeral.

I had my lunch with the Sarge and then busied myself with paperwork for an hour. I walked up to the funeral from the station and made sure I was up at the church a good half hour before the allotted start time of 3.00pm.

I was amazed at how many people were already there and already sitting down. A lot of the Chinese smoked cigarettes and they were happy to go and occupy their seats until they had someone sat next to them and then they would nip out of the church for a fag. I was surprised that the already overcrowded church was so well respected in that if someone had claimed a chair, it was respected.

I was stood by the church front door when Ki San Wang approached me and ushered me forward to sit in the second row. I had never met any of Shi Low's family so I did not know anyone immediately surrounding me. I was looking around when the gentleman next to me was trying to attract my attention. He explained, in very good English, that he was to be my interpreter for the ceremony. If I preferred he would stay silent until I asked for him to translate anything.

The church was well occupied to overflowing. I could not begin to guess how many people were inside. I would hazard a guess at over 500 but it would be a guess. As I looked around the church I happened to see the Boss sat on the back row. He had managed to get a seat and would be able to enjoy the ceremony. Assuming, that is, he wanted to see the spectacle of a Chinese funeral and he was not there only because he had been invited and it would have been considered rude to decline the invitation.

The church was well filled when we got the nod to rise as the coffin was carried in. There was a local priest in attendance as well as a Chinese priest. Between them they managed to get though the opening few words and I got the gist that the ceremony would be conducted in Chinese as well as English in accord with Shi Low's wishes.

I settled down and was quite prepared to get up when asked and sit down when asked. My interpreter was poised at my side but very respectful in that he would wait to be asked before he translated anything.

The service got underway and I was surprised at it being such a joyous service. It was filled with people being happy that Shi Low had gone to the afterlife, and it was a genuine case that he had gone on to better things and not just sad that he had left his life here. There was a time for people to get up and say he was a great guy and I was pleased that so many of his countrymen were given a chance to speak in preference to the assembled big wigs. Obviously there were a few bigwigs that had the chance to have their say but for me it was the assembled small folk that made my day, the everyday shopkeepers who got up and said something nice. Shi Low was well respected in his community but he was also well loved because of the way he carried out his duties. I also discovered that Shi Low was aged 75. He looked remarkably fit for his age.

The translator did not have much to say as I didn't really ask him much. I got a strong sense of the speakers that Shi Low was well liked and it showed in the way the mourners looked down at his coffin and smiled. Often they would bow to the coffin as their way of showing respect. I quite liked that side of their religion. Eventually there had to be formalities and the way the two faiths allowed each other to do their bit was amazing and it was also very peaceful.

At the conclusion of the ceremony Ki San Wang approached and said they would consider it a great honour if the Detective Inspector and I would join them for refreshments afterwards. When I went through to the ante room there was mountains of food for people to eat. Everyone had brought something along to assist Shi Low's being ready for his next journey. If I got anything wrong in my description, I apologise but that was as close as I could understand the ceremony. The translator did his duty and stayed by the DI and myself for the whole after match ceremony. Apologies, that sounds a little disrespectful but it says what I mean. This was a happy occasion and we had every right to be enjoying the passing of a good man.

By now it was well after 6.00pm. The ceremony had gone a little late as there were so many people who wanted to say a few words and then there was the whole issue of there being two faiths present and they both needed to say their piece.

I guess the Boss and I left sometime before seven and we walked back to the station together to get our vehicles. The Boss reckoned if he had to go, he wouldn't mind it being the Chinese way. They were far happier about the whole thing.

I got home at 7.15 and I wanted to talk to someone about my experience. I wanted to ring Bernie but I was a little hesitant. Usually she rang me but she didn't, so I didn't. I went to sleep at peace and was awake bright and early in the morning.

Tuesday

A gloomy looking day and I had missed the weather forecast the previous evening. In at my usual time and the first person I saw was the Sarge. He handed me my coffee and then said, "You better sit down. Tohi was topped last night. On Te Ngae Road. No, it was off Te Ngae Road on Brent Road. Just past the Regency Park, just before you get to Walnut Place, just by the school. He was taken off his bike by a bullet. That's all I know. They got hold of Bernie and Derek because they couldn't get hold of you and the Boss. Hang on, here's the Boss I need to tell him as well."

There was a reason the office could not get hold of me. Everyone was sternly admonished to turn off their cell phones at the beginning of the service. The Chinese, for the most part had already turned their phones off. The rest of us had to be reminded and we did so.

The three of us went into the Boss's office and the Sarge relayed the news. The Boss was all business and he shouted out for Derek and Bernie. The Sarge reckoned because they had been out until after 7.00 last night he reckoned the Boss would have told them to come in late, so when they rang the Sarge as the highest ranking and available CIB officer he had told them not to come in until 9.00am. They had tidied up as much of the paperwork as they could and waited for the ambulance to take Tohi up to the morgue and they had gone home. Neither had got home until nearly eight pm having been called out when the incident was occurring, the information for which was received at the callout room at 5.19pm.

The Boss and I finished our coffee and headed out to the scene of the crime. It looked like it was a pro hit. The assassin had parked at the end of Brent Road in the grass. He had waited for Tohi to crest the rise in the road and taken him down with a clean shot in the chest. He had fallen off his bike and been dragged along the road until he and the bike parted company. We went up to the grassy field and had a scout around. We found the site where the guy had waited and with a further cast around we found the cartridge case. I made a mental note that it looked like a .357 with a centre fire action on the bolt. I bagged the shell case and carried on scouting around. The hit man had picked his spot well. He was surrounded by grass that was a couple of feet high and he had cleared a path in front of him so he had a clear shot down Brent Road. The Boss did some checking on his phone and found that Tohi had a home on Walnut Place and was probably heading home.

Over the phone he was also told that someone had reported a trailbike that had been set ablaze around a couple of kilometers away on the Tarawera Road. Evidently the fire brigade had been called out and quickly doused the fire but there was no chance of getting anything like fingerprints off the burned remains. After we had searched the scene and found nothing that Derek and Bernie had not found already, we went off to the Tarawera Road and examined the burnt out bike. As far as I could tell it was the burnt out remains of the 250cc Kawasaki I had been to the incident report of a couple of weeks ago. I felt reasonable about tidying up loose ends but I still had the feeling that the gang war would break out again. The Boss and I discussed the incident and we both decided that Ronnie may have had something to do with Tohi's death. Let's be honest, Ronnie was our prime suspect!

I personally did not want Ronnie to be involved as I wanted this whole gang war to be over with. The Boss and I phoned Ronnie and said we were on our way. Ronnie seemed cheerful and said he would put the jug on.

We pulled up at the Gang HQ on View Road. We waited for the car to be pulled back and went inside where Ronnie was awaiting us.

"Whoa, hey, Sarge, you bought the Boss around. I'm not in trouble, am I?"

There was something about Ronnie's attitude that struck a chord with us both. Ronnie seemed to be his usual cheerful self. Why was he not acting suspicious and waiting for us to ask him troubling questions?

The Boss and I glanced at each other as we walked up the stairs. Something was not quite right.

We sat down and Ronnie made us a cuppa. When he had sat down with us we started asking questions.

The Boss started with, "Ronnie, we are here investigating the death of Tohi, your opposite number in the Black Power gang. Where were you between 5.00 and 5.30 last evening?"

Ronnie was blown away. I could see he was genuinely shocked and I knew we were looking up the wrong tree. "Tohi is dead? Well it had nothing to do with me. What happened?"

The Boss continued, "He was killed last evening as he went to his home. I ask again. Where were you between 5.00 and 5.30?"

"Playing with the kids. The missus brought them round here and I was having a... at 5.30 I was reading to them. Let me think. At 5.00 we were watching a Peppa Pig DVD. Am I a suspect?"

I interjected, "Ronnie, you are our prime bloody suspect! Of anyone we know, you wanted him dead the most. Do you have anyone who can corroborate your story?"

Ronnie was a mixture of being pleased he had an alibi and I could also see his mind was working as to how he could profit from the situation. I had known Ronnie for so long I could nearly tell how his mind worked.

"Last night at 5.00. Butch was here, the missus, the oh, and Jimmy, Ray and Dave were here. Outside on guard was. Hey Butch, who pulled guard last night?"

The answer came back that Ray, the other one, Murph and Tane were on guard last night.

Ronnie repeated the info to the Boss.

The Boss was his usual self and he told Ronnie, "Sod it! You were our favourite suspect. Now we have to go and do some work. Drink your tea, DS. We still have work to do!"

The Boss could be refreshingly honest and with Ronnie it was always best to talk simply so there was no misunderstanding.

Ronnie was still asking questions about how Tohi had died. The Boss gave him as much info as he felt like giving and then we left and went back to the station.

The Sarge was waiting for us, "I thought you might have Ronnie in cuffs. What happened?"

The Boss and I looked at each other. We both were of the same opinion that Ronnie had nothing to do with Tohi's death. The three of us sat in the bull pen. Derek and Bernie had been given the cases from the squad room and were out dealing with them.

"Okay," said the Sarge, "If Ronnie says he had nothing to do with it, who is next on the list? Would it have something to do with Shi Low's death? It might have something to do with that guy Tananga."

Just then Bernie and Derek walked in together and joined us. They were asked what they had uncovered the previous evening when they had gone to Tohi's shooting.

Between them they had basically done the paperwork and sent the body off to the morgue. By the time they were finished it was getting late and darkness was falling which made it hard to do anything more. It also explained why they had not discovered the scene where the shooter had lain in wait.

The Boss told how we had gone to the scene of the motorcycle being burned and said it looked like someone was covering up any evidence. He surmised that the bike may have been used as a getaway vehicle. A lightweight trail bike would have been ideal for getting away across the fields and into the forest. We agreed that this was probably the likely case. The Sarge was up at the whiteboard by now and suggested we put our heads together.

He put the heading of 'Tohi's death' across the top and then we brainstormed.

Among the suggestions for further discussion were:

Tananga's death.

Shi Low's death.

Chinese involvement

Ronnie being involved or the Mongrel Mob.

A revolt among the Black Power mob.

Someone else?

Drug sales. Tohi's increased involvement among Ronnie's clients.

Jacko? His business was suffering from the increased watchfulness of the security guys.

By now we were getting stuck for ideas so we went back to the headings and worked them further.

Tananga's death. Could be a revenge hit by the Auckland gangs. Tohi was known as the opposition, so why did they all drive out to Ronnie's Gang HQ to pay their respects to Tananga. It just seemed a bit odd.

Shi Low's death. A definite starter. The Chinese community were known for revenge but usually they waited for a while. Revenge is a dish best served cold was their saying. Would they have reacted so quickly to avenge Shi Low's death, if it was indeed Tohi who had planned that death. Did we have any evidence to suggest Tohi was involved with Shi Low dying? No, we did not. Ki San Wang had already said there would be no retribution for the death of Shi Low until after the funeral. I reckoned the funeral would have been done with by 5.00. Yes there was the usual feed afterwards but did Ki San Wang really have the guts to order a kill on Tohi so soon after the funeral?

Ronnie being involved. Certainly a motive to act but then Ronnie had definitely seemed surprised at Tohi's death. We knew that Ronnie denied everything. Was it likely one of his underlings had acted as an individual. The Boss and I agreed that it was unlikely anyone would act without Ronnie's say so. Between us, we were still of the opinion that Ronnie may be innocent in this case.

A revolt among the Black Power Mob. Unlikely. We would have heard if anyone wanted a revolt from the boss. Tohi ruled his roost with a rod of fear. Most of the gang members were new so would still be loyal to Tohi. Of all of the scenarios we figured this was the least likely.

Someone else? We were aware that the Highway 51 were trying to get established in Rotorua, as were the Comancheros. Would either of them have had the guts to pull something major off like this? Perhaps while they thought Tohi's attention was solely fixed on the Mongrel Mob. Again we figured this was an unlikely scene so we crossed it off.

Drug sales. We had heard that Ronnie was getting squeezed by Tohi out of some of his regular drug clientele. Was this an attempt by Ronnie to right the wrong. In this case we would have another major gang war on our hands which could go on until one of the gangs emerged victorious. As both of the gangs were about even in numbers was this a likely scenario? We figured it was something we had to be aware of and left it in the mix.

We also discussed the Issue of who should approach the Chinese and see if they had any involvement with the Tohi's death. It was agreed that I should make the approach. I already had a reasonable relationship with Ki San Wang and it was felt that I should make the initial approach and call the Boss in if I had any suspicions.

The Boss and I retreated to his office and had a further chat. Mike had made a comment that he thought that Bernie and I may be an item. It was something Bernie had said while they were on a case together. I had my money on Tim discovering us as an item and the Boss reckoned it would be Derek as he had gotten to work with me a little recently. As it was, no money changed hands and Mike was asked to keep his mouth quiet about Bernie and I. We also talked about whether it was appropriate for us to approach the Comancheros or the Highway 51 lads. The issue was that if we made the approach it almost acknowledged we were aware of their presence. It was decided between us we should not approach them as a couple of gangs in town were enough for us to acknowledge.

That left me to approach the Chinese and see if they had anything to do with Tohi's death. They were beginning to look like our main suspects but I was still convinced they would have waited for a while before acting. I said I would go and see Ki San Wang if he had not called me in a couple of days.

Given that it was virtually common knowledge Bernie and I were an item I subtly mentioned to Bernie we had a date and where were we going. She invited me up to her place and told me that bed was probably not an option but she would make me a nice meal as compensation. I was happy enough with that and then Bernie had to go out on a call and Mike from the morgue rang to tell us his prelim report was ready for us.

I told the Boss and we went up to the morgue together and had a chat with Mike while we were there. It was always interesting talking to Mike as he looked at things in a different manner than we did.

He reckoned the hit was professional. A bullet, a .357 right to the centre of the heart mass and Tohi would have been dead the moment the bullet hit him. No indications of alcohol but a tox screen would be needed to confirm that. A lot of damage to the skin with abrasions from when he still had contact with the bike but he was convinced that Tohi would have been dead as soon as the bullet hit him. The Boss had already had a forensics report on Tohi's motorcycle. No bullet wound but the bike was pretty much a write off as it had been extensively damaged on contact with the road.

With that we were only waiting for the tox report to tidy up the paperwork. Mike said he should have that back by tomorrow and he would email it to us. The Boss dropped me off at my motor and I went home. I did get a call from Bernie that night which was nice but we mainly chatted about how our day had been.

Wednesday

A nice day but I was still thinking about who would have wanted Tohi dead. I know we had almost discounted Ronnie but it was still uppermost when I walked into the station. The Sarge, as always, was ready with my coffee. The Boss was running late so the Sarge and I joined Derek and Mike and Bernie in the bull pen. The Sarge had already got the cases from the Squad room and was waiting to hand them out to whoever turned up. He had three cases and there were three detectives so he got rid of them quite easily. We all sat and drank our drinks and chewed the fat until perhaps 8.30 when the Boss walked in and every one of the DC's scarpered or tried to look busy.

"Sorry, DS. The Boss wanted me to go up to his office and tell me what there was to know about Tohi. It made the papers and he has been asked for a quote on who we reckon did it. They were trying to get him to say it was all part of the gang war but at least he's too smart to fall for that one! He's probably up there now talking to the local rag and saying no comment and our investigations are proceeding. The usual stuff. Morning, Sarge, anything come over from the Squaddies?"

"The usual. Three cases and there are three DC's so it's all in hand."

Then he turned to me, "Not heard anything from your Chinese bloke, the new boss?"

"Not yet. If I haven't heard today I'll get on the phone to him tomorrow."

"Make it today! We only have him left on the suspect list for Tohi."

"Will do, Boss."

"What else have we got to keep us busy?" The Boss was in a good mood and it showed. But when he was in this kind of mood he wanted things to happen and he wanted them to happen now!

"Okay, DS. We have sod all on our plate. What say we go and follow up or give assistance to the DC's?"

We worked out where the three DC's would be and we went out to Malfroy Road for a domestic burglary. The homeowner was pleased to see that we had allocated the top brass to their case. Derek was not quite so happy but he made the best of it and introduced us to Mrs. Homeowner.

The Boss made a few suggestions which Derek had already thought of and then we went to see Bernie's case.

Bernie had a domestic assault by the husband on the wife. She was trying to build up the trust between her and the wife. Having a couple of guys walk in did not do a lot for her situation. She took us outside and explained what she was doing and politely asked us to sod off!

By the time we caught up with Mike he had already dealt with his case and was back at the station. He had asked the print lads to go round and do their thing. After that we had to wait for a repeat offence or hope the guy was already on our list for other crimes.

We had been out a little over an hour and we had covered the three cases. Now the Boss wanted something else to do. Just as he was bleating about how the Rotorua Crims should pace themselves a little better, the Sarge's phone had rung. KI San Wang would like me to visit this afternoon. Would 3.00 be convenient. The Sarge passed the enquiry on to me and I said I would be delighted to see him at 3.00.

The Boss looked at me as if to say, 'Didn't I tell you to ring him?' Then he turned away and went into his office.

Never mind I would meet Ki San Wang at 3.00 this afternoon and finish off my questions about Tohi.

Chapter 9

I went to see Ki San Wang and as always I was punctual. The mahjong players were once again playing in the room as I passed through. It seemed to me that a great man had passed and yet here was life going on as normal.

I was ushered into a comfortable seat and Ki San Wang immediately offered me a cup of tea which I graciously accepted. When we were both sat down Ki Wan Sang asked me if I had any questions I would like to ask him.

I was at a loss as I was unsure whether he meant questions about the funeral or whatever.

I used my gut hunch that he would not be inviting me for tea merely to pass the time. So went straight in with, "May I ask if you or your family may have had something to do with the death of Tohi, the gang leader who was killed on Monday evening?"

With that question asked I sat back and sipped my tea.

He thought for a moment and then spoke," Are you asking the most appropriate questions, Detective Sergeant?"

He had me back on the ropes. I thought about it for a second and then asked, "What have you done about the passing of Shi Low?"

Again he thought for a moment before saying, "You may have to think of a bigger picture when you ask your questions."

I was definitely flummoxed so I asked him what would be a good question to ask.

He seemed pleased, "That is more of a general question, but if you were perhaps to ask me about the passing of the gentleman from

Auckland. I believe he was called Tananga. Then I may be able to speak wisely with you. Please ask me a further question, Detective Sergeant."

"Ki San Wang. May I ask you about the death of Tananga. He was a good, er, man from Auckland City."

"Unfortunately, Detective Sergeant, you were perhaps one of the few who may have held that opinion. I am told that in Auckland he was known as being a quite violent man. Reports of his deeds would not support your claim that he was a good man."

"May I ask who would want to see Tananga injured."

"Detective Sergeant, anything I may say will probably be denied by myself should it be repeated outside of my office. Given that you are aware of this possibility, do you wish to continue with your questions?"

I nodded but Ki San Wang needed me to say I understood. I said I would agree to whatever he wanted to say to me.

He took that as a yes. "Detective Sergeant, there was already a price on the head of Tananga from my Auckland friends. While I do not wish to participate in the crimes from another region, Shi Low had been approached by, let us say friends of the family, to allow them to deal with Tananga while he was less heavily protected by his colleagues, here in Rotorua. We have a gentleman from Taupo who is capable of dealing with such a man. We were only an intermediary in the transaction but I must insist that Tananga was not the, I believe you called him a 'good man'. I am told from reliable sources that may have been better suited to your other friends."

"So you were a part of, what, dealing with the Tananga problem?"

"Merely an intermediary."

"I see." I sipped at my teas as I tried to make sense of what I was hearing. My teacup was empty!

Ki San Wang immediately asked if I required a top up. I said yes to give me a few more seconds to think.

I thanked Ki San Wang for the second cup of tea and wondered what my next question should be. I looked at him and he smiled back at me as if to say, 'your move, buddy!'

Then I had the brainwave. Well, it was for me! "If I were to ask another question, what should that question relate to?"

"Perhaps you could ask about the death of Shi Low?"

"Ki San Wang. How does this whole gang war relate to the death of Shi Low?"

He replied," Ah, yes, a great man and well loved by everyone who knew him well. There is one person who may have born him Ill will. I am led to believe that the people who attempted to injure your friend who you like to call Ronnie had been, shall we say rounded up and handed over to the Police. I understand they sang like the proverbial canary when they were questioned. It is possible you may have even benefitted from their willingness to talk to you?"

I agreed that might have happened.

Ki San Wang continued, "Unfortunately the person who bore ill will to our friend, Shi Low, tried to ensure that Shi Low was harmed. Unfortunately Shi Low remained unharmed but Shi Low's good friend was injured as a result. Seeing such a good friend injured meant that Shi Low possibly had to make some accommodations with the people who wished him ill. Notwithstanding the accommodations made, obviously Shi Low was forced to deal with those youths who tried to injure him. Sadly they will not be able to offer harm to any other person."

"I am impressed that Shi Low showed such forgiveness under such trying circumstances."

"It was just one part of Shi Low's forgiving nature."

"You were going to mention the accident suffered by Shi Low."

"Ah, yes. Unfortunately you may remember the gentleman from Taupo who we may employ occasionally?"

"The Hit man!"

"Detective Sergeant, Shi Low was quite correct, on the occasion you may speak like a civilised person and in the next breath you resort to crude and quite unnecessary banalities."

"I apologise for my clumsiness. Please continue." Yeah I had overstepped the mark with my last remark. I was really out of my depth with this conversation. All of this talk about getting a hit man to do the dirty work was beyond my comprehension.

"As I was saying. There are few people in the area who may have the skills to execute such a mission that requires such finesse. We have a man in Taupo. It would appear he is not exclusive to us. He was hired by someone to take out Shi Low's new vehicle. If the first shot at the tyre had failed he had been instructed to place the next bullet in the chest of the driver. Would the man in Taupo have taken on the task if he knew who the victim was? We shall probably never know but the man was skilled in his aim and Shi Low died within seconds of the bullet hitting the vehicle. For that we shall be ever grateful."

"So you.... Hang on I am confused. I offer my apologies but who organised the attack on Shi Low?"

"Perhaps you should ask a further question, Detective Sergeant. A good question might be posed as to why Tohi should be singled out."

I was struggling but I still knew how to play this game. "Ki San Wang. May I be permitted to enquire as to why Tohi was executed?"

"That is a good question, Detective Sergeant. Shi Low had called the leader of the Black Power gang and they had spoken at some length. The result of this discussion was perhaps relating to the disposal of the two men who had aimed a shotgun at the car Shi Low was driving. Shi Low had them quickly off their motorcycle and he managed to get the associates away from the scene of the incident. They were later questioned at the home of one of our people where they confessed that Your colleague Tohi..."

"Not my colleague, but please carry on."

"A clumsy choice of word, for which I offer my apology. Tohi was found to be the organizer of the attack on Shi Low. The two men who carried out the attack on Shi Low were disposed of and a phone call was made to Tohi. During the course of this call Tohi agreed to cease any further action against Shi Low or any member of our community. You may recall that when you called Shi Low later that day he assumed you were wrong in your assertion of an attack on his vehicle. That is because Shi Low believed he had reached an agreement with Tohi about there being no further retribution looked for.

"I do recall having a conversation with Shi Low and I assumed it had been dealt with."

"Detective Sergeant, a man has only two things he can honour personally. That is his word and his reputation. By arranging for the man from Taupo to attack Shi Low less than a week later showed that Tohi could not be trusted. It was arranged for the man from Taupo to do to this Tohi what had been done to Shi Low. Now, if you have no further questions?"

"Hang on. I mean I may have some further questions to ask Ki San Wang, if I may."

He nodded to affirm he was willing to answer some more questions.

"Tohi was killed by the guy from Taupo, the same guy that killed Shi Low, who was killed because he had the guys who attacked his car handed over to the law."

Ki San Wang thought for a moment before answering, "That is a generality but it does serve the purpose."

"And the... So the stolen motorcycle was used for his getaway and then had to be torched."

"That is how it happened; I believe."

"And the Gang war?"

"I would assume that is over. If your colleague, Ronnie, was clever enough he would offer a truce to get them to come over to his side. But

I am unaware of the codes between these gangs so that is not for me to say."

I sat and thought for a few seconds. Ki San Wang allowed me to think. I had finished my second cup of tea so I prepared an exit speech.

"Ki San Wang, as always it has been an illuminating discussion. As always I do not expect any of this conversation to repeated between ourselves and as always, thank you for the refreshing cup of tea."

I stood up as did Ki San Wang. "Detective Sergeant, as always I thank you for your company. You know, we may make a civilised person out of you, yet". I knew he was joking but I also think I had passed a test by understanding what he was trying to say without saying actually anything.

As I left his office, Ki San Wang loosed another remark, "Detective Sergeant, you did not ask about our friend from Taupo?"

I stopped and asked him, "May I ask what happened to him?"

"Such a man is to be respected. He did not know Shi Low was the intended target. Such a good man should be respected. He still is."

"Thank you again for your hospitality Ki San Wang." I almost bowed to him as you would a revered and wiser gentleman. I caught myself in time.

Ki San Wang gave me a cheery wave and just said, "Anytime." Was he having a chuckle at my expense?

Chapter 10

I walked back to the Station and I was pensive. I had taken on a whole load of information from Ki San Wang and I knew it was important that I not forget anything of our conversation.

When I walked into the station, the Boss was away so I said I would hold off telling the Sarge until the Boss returned.

Within a few minutes the Boss returned and we settled in his office.

I tried to recall every detail of my previous conversation.

"Right" I started, "Tananga was knocked off by a guy in Taupo." The Boss and the Sarge looked concerned.

I continued, "As I understand it there's a bloke in Taupo who is a hit man for hire. I don't know what he charges but Tananga had upset the families in Auckland, the Chinese families, and they wanted him dealt to while he had less people around him in Rotorua. I believe the locals organised to make contact with the guy from Taupo but after that it was between him and the Auckland families. Any questions so far?"

Neither of them had a question so I continued, "As far as I can tell, Shi Low and Tohi had a word and Tohi agreed not to seek further revenge against Shi Low and we ended up getting those lads into custody. Speaking of which, when is their trial date?"

The Sarge reckoned it was not for at least two months as the courts were backed up. There was some issue in that the two guys wanted their admission read out in court. As far as I could tell they wanted Shi Low, or his successor to know what they were admitting to.

"Right, then, you remember I had a word with Shi Low and he reckoned I was dreaming when I said he had a shotgun that took out his windscreen, out on Pukehangi Road."

The Boss remembered as he and I had gone out to the scene.

"Right, I might be reading between the lines here but the first go at Shi Low was an amateur affair. Shi Low got the lads who did it and we got them eventually. It turns out that Tohi also used the guy from Taupo and organised him to have a go at Shi Low. We know he was successful and he also wrote off a nice new Mercedes."

The Boss made a comment about the guy from Taupo being a busy guy. I had no further thoughts on the subject so I carried on.

"And now we get to Tohi. Ki San Wang reckons the only thing a bloke has is his reputation and his word. Because Tohi had another go at Shi Low they reckoned he was not a guy to be trusted so they also got the guy from Taupo up to have a go at Tohi. That brings up to today. Right, questions?"

"So they also had the same guy from Taupo topped for shooting Shi Low?" asked the Sarge.

"No. They reckon he knew nothing about the hit on Shi Low only that he had to take out a nice brand new Merc. They also reckon he is very good so they let him live and they reckon they will use him again."

The Sarge asked again, "So this guy took out Tananga first?"

"Correct. They reckon Tananga was a right villain on his own patch and it was too good a chance to miss when he was down here and not totally surrounded by his men."

The questions continued for around twenty minutes before they had exhausted my brain and memory. I took a look at my watch and it was already 5.20. I needed to get home and have a shower before my date tonight. The Boss saw me looking at my watch and told me to bugger off home. Also, he told me not to tell Bernie about my conversation. This needed the Boss to consult with the big Boss and that would not happen until the morning.

Let me say I had a very pleasant evening with Bernie. We sat and ate the meal she had cooked and then watched the box for a while until I kissed her good night. All of the while I wanted to tell her about my chat with Ki San Wang but I was restricted by what the Boss had said.

Thursday

On the Thursday I was in a good mood. The weather was fine and I had had a very nice kiss from Bernie, last night, that promised something more.

The Boss was waiting in the office when I walked in and that was unexpected. He had to wait until 8.30am before the big Boss was free. He went upstairs and I settled down to have my coffee with the Sarge. Then the phone rang and I was also summoned upstairs to see the Boss and the big Boss.

I recited my story from yesterday while the Boss sat and listened.

Then I was kept up there while the Boss and the big Boss argued back and forth.

Could they leak something to the papers about the gang war being over. No!

Could they subpoena Ki San Wang to tell what he knew under oath? Again that was met with another no as he would simply deny everything.

Should we tell Ronnie, as this information may help if they could persuade Ronnie to take over the BP lads. Another resounding no, as the last thing they wanted was a gang of Mob members that now was doubled in size.

The upshot was that we had all of the news related to me yesterday that we just could not use. We could not even call the cases closed without someone being prosecuted.

The big Boss said he would think about it and get back to the Boss if he had any ideas.

As far as the Boss was concerned he had done the right thing and told the big Boss. It was up to him how he dealt with the crimes stats.

Interestingly when the Boss and I got back downstairs the Sarge and the Boss went into his office but I was excluded. I didn't care as I had done my duty as far as anyone was concerned. I still wanted to tell Bernie though, but that was also not on the cards.

Eventually the Sarge got up and left the Boss's office and he called me in.

"Sorry about that, The Sarge had something he wanted to talk to me about. Now what are we going to tell Ronnie? You can't tell him it was your Chinese mate. But you should tell him he's not on our suspect list for Tohi."

"I'll tell him something. I'd better go and see him so he knows he's off our list."

I rang Ronnie and said I was on my way. He said he'd put a brew on and had I got anyone for Tohi? I told him I would tell him all when I got there.

For the first time in a month or so there was no car across the inner gate when I rolled up although it was put back in place when I entered.

Ronnie greeted me, "No grapes and no handcuffs. I must have been a good lad!"

I shook his hand and we went upstairs and had a brew. I told Ronnie we were looking for a guy in Taupo for the death of Tohi. He was happy he was off the hook for it and I declined to answer any of his questions about this guy in Taupo. Ronnie did not need to know we would probably never get the guy from Taupo unless we got a really good lead on him.

I left Ronnie after about a half hour and wondered where I should go next. The Gang war seems to have fairly passed us by without too much peripheral damage. I suppose the local paper will get onto it the next time they are stuck for something to write about. I satisfied myself with thinking that was something for the local reporter and the CI to worry about. I was too far down the chain of command to be worried by those people.

What else happened? Oh eventually the two guys who made the attempt on Ronnie were hauled up to court. The CP did his best but the best he could get was wounding with intent. The other guy was also charged with the same offence as he was driving what was considered to be the getaway vehicle. They both got 5 years for wounding. They will probably be out in three if they behave.

My rapist had been quiet for a over a month. He did surface again in the Western Heights area but the Sarge reckoned that rapists come and go. They might be active for a month or so and then get in a relationship where they behave for a few months. We may still get the guy as at least we had a DNA sample from him.

Nothing more was done about the shootings of Tananga and Shi Low and Tohi. As far as we were concerned they would stay on the books until they were considered a cold case.

Ki San Wang became something of a person of interest as he reckoned that Shi Low had done things the old fashioned way and he wanted to 'update' their image. He was someone I was told to keep an eye on over the next few months.

As for me, and Bernie, still an item but we haven't moved in together yet. I haven't seen Janet for over a month. Maybe I should go and see her and apologise. Maybe I'll go and see her as a CI. I'd better warn her that is why I am coming. It definitely wouldn't do for me to turn up and she is starker's. No, that wouldn't do at all. It might give me a few problems I am not ready to deal with yet.

Chapter 11

That night was unusual for Huia. Normally if she was line dancing her hubby might have someone around for a bit of company. Tonight was not her line dancing night and her hubby had invited the DI from work. Oddly she had not been invited to join in with their talk. She busied herself in the kitchen while the two men chatted in the lounge.

Colin: Don't tell me not to worry. This is serious!

Dave: Think about it, if this new bloke with the Chinese was serious he would have done something by now.

Colin: What was our income from Ronnie last month?

Dave: Just shy of seven grand. Don't forget he was under pressure from Tohi putting on the squeeze and then he had his arm broken.

Colin: Seven grand's not bad but we used to get over nine as an average. Is Ronnie fiddling us?

Dave: No, I reckon Ronnie knows which side his bread is buttered. Ronnie knows to be straight with us.

Colin: Any news on who will take over the Black Power?

Dave: The favourite is the guy from Cambridge. If they merge the gangs they might be a power. Somehow I can't see it happening and if they do it will probably be in Cambridge.

Colin: Worth having a word with the guy from Cambridge?

Dave: Already in hand. I've been on the phone and told him we can offer protection. He reckons he won't need it but if we bust a few of his drug drops he will come round to our way of thinking.

Colin: Have you met the new guy from the Chinese yet?

Dave: He is called Ki San Wang. I reckon our first visit should be from you. They do like it when you send someone high ranking. It gives them face; Mark was telling me. Watch out for this new bloke. Something tells me he won't be as easygoing as Shi Low was.

Colin: And Mark is the only one who has seen the new bloke?

Dave: Yeah, but I reckon he's having second thoughts about maintaining contact. Said he felt a bit odd when the Chinese was talking about having blokes bumped off. Speaking of second thoughts, have you had any more thoughts about who will replace Mark as the head of the Vice Squad?

Colin: Not yet, it has to be someone of senior rank. How about if I make Bernie his deputy? She is a higher rank but not high enough, and I reckoned she'd be perfect to check he wasn't backsliding and seeing that Janet again. Matter of fact I reckon that might be a good idea. Maybe I'll mention it to him tomorrow.

And that is where we shall leave the two friends having a quiet drink together.

<u>Other work by the same Author</u>

Police series

A series about crime in 'Rotorua'

Book1 <u>The Panel</u>

It seems there is a 'panel' of people in Rotorua who decides if the local court system is giving a fair shake to the local criminals. If they get off lightly there may be further retribution available.

Book 2 <u>The Party</u>

A party takes place out in Hamurana area and the next day there is a murder case at the same address. Coincidence? Or is there more than meets the eye?

Book 3 <u>The Judge</u>

We appear to have a moral guardian at work. Then there is also another guy committing the same crime. Coincidence or not?

Book 4 <u>The War</u>

It's finally happened, and a gang war breaks out. The last thing the Police need is for someone else to get involved. And the last thing the Police need, is always exactly what happens!

Book 5 <u>The payoff.</u>

It's a time when people need to decide who is on their side. And who can be let go? It's time for all friendships to be tested!

SOUL PURPOSE

Vol 1 & 11 & 111

A fiction work with something of a twist

He has returned.

The subtitle is "and it's so not what you think" Probably one of the most fun books I have written and probably the most amusing. The Son of God has returned, and he finds the world is in something of a state. Partly because of what he said and did a couple of thousand years ago on his last visit here. Yeah, it's all a bit confused now he is back. Let's see how he deals with it!

Mickey Carter: An angel with L-plates

It's funny and set in South Manchester. It's easy being an angel. Isn't it?

I have Angels at my table.

An interesting story set in England as natural disasters occur and somehow the higher levels of heaven are involved.

Danny Casanova's legacy

A fun story centred around a young guys first venture into the world of grownups and doing what grownups do. Or at least trying to!

Time and time again.

A book about past life experiences. Interestingly it only deals with past lives on planet earth.

About the Author

Andy has been writing for the last twenty years and has written a number of books over a wide variety of genre. His first book Sold over 5000 copies and he continues to write on whatever the mood takes him. Currently he is finishing Books on the crime scene in Rotorua, New Zealand. As always his books are not meant to be taken seriously. If you haven't laughed today, read one of Andy's books!